SLEUTH'S ALCHEMY

SLEUTH'S ALCHEMY

Cases of Mrs. Bradley and Others

By Gladys Mitchell

Edited by Nicholas Fuller

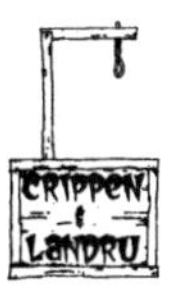

Crippen & Landru, Publishers
Norfolk, Virginia
2005

Published by permission of Gregory & Company, Authors' Agents,
London

We are grateful to B.A. Pike and to John Cooper for copies of the stories

Cover and dust jacket illustration by Gail Cross
"Lost Classics" cover design by Deborah Miller

Crippen & Landru logo by Eric Greene

Lost Classics logo by Eric Greene, based on a design by Ike Morgan,
ca. 1895

ISBN (cloth edition): 1-932009-30-2
ISBN (trade edition): 1-932009-31-0

FIRST EDITION

Crippen & Landru Publishers
P.O. Box 9315
Norfolk, VA 23505
USA

www.crippenlandru.com
info@crippenlandru.com

Contents

Gladys Mitchell:

The Body of Her Work

Imagine: a drought-stricken and backward village in rural Hampshire, where aeroplanes are regarded as the tool of the Devil, where half the inhabitants indulge in pagan rituals straight out of the *Golden Bough*, where a visiting writer is believed to be the "long, thin man" who sleeps in the barrow, and the murderer of three people — a sadist, schizophrenic and maniac — is revealed to be the Devil.

Then there is the remarkable case at Chaynings, where a world-renowned explorer, drowned in a bathtub, turns out to be a woman — much to the horror of his (her?) fiancée, who promptly goes mad and starts smashing clocks and stabbing people before being put out of everybody else's misery by the psycho-analyst staying in the house — a woman who is arrested, acquitted, and goes on to appear in a further 65 novels. Or the case where a corpse on the railway line turns out not to have been there at all, but was seen only because the witness had second sight; or the repeated sightings of a naiad in the River Itchen, Winchester; or an attempt to re-enact the Mysteries of Eleusis which ends disastrously when a severed head is found among the Aesculapian snakes.

Many readers will have begun to wonder what asylum the author of these books escaped from. Others, however, will recognise from these descriptions the work of Gladys Mitchell, school-teacher, historical novelist (as Stephen Hockaby), detective novelist (who also wrote as Malcolm Torrie) and creator of the indomitable psychiatrist-detective Mrs. Bradley, the heroine of 66 novels. Mitchell also wrote some 31 short stories, all, with one exception, published in *The Evening Standard*, primarily between 1950 and 1953, when that quality London evening newspaper was commissioning short stories by other celebrated detective writers such as Josephine Bell, Edmund Crispin, Michael Gilbert, Cyril Hare, Michael Innes, E. R. Punshon and Julian Symons. Mitchell's stories have not been collected hitherto. In this volume they appear together for the first time.

The Writer

Mitchell was born in the village of Cowley, Oxfordshire in 1901 (where she set her 1936 novel *Dead Men's Morris* and her 1976 novel *Late, Late in the Evening*). Her family subsequently moved to London and then to the Middlesex village of Brentford, which she used as the setting of *The Rising of the Moon* (1945). She was educated at the Green School, Isleworth, Middlesex, graduating in 1918. Between 1919 and 1921, she studied to become a teacher at Goldsmith's College, University of London, and gained an external diploma in history from University College, London in 1926. She specialised in "English and history, swimming and games,"[1] and returned to Brentford, teaching at St. Paul's School from 1921 to 1925, and Senior Girls' School from 1941 to 1950. She also taught at St. Ann's Senior Girls' School, Ealing (1925–39), and the Matthew Arnold School, Staines, Middlesex, from 1953 until her retirement in 1961, after which she lived in the Dorset village of Corfe Mullen until her death on 27 July 1983.[2]

Her companion for much of her life was Winifred Blazey, who wrote her own detective stories and may, as the joint dedication (with "Pam") of *Groaning Spinney* (1950) suggests, have collaborated in a few of Mitchell's novels. Another writing friend was Helen Simpson, perhaps better-known today for the Hitchcock film *Under Capricorn* than for her stories featuring the actor-sleuth Sir John Saumarez (one of which Hitchcock filmed as *Murder*) or for her collaboration with Dorothy L. Sayers over the play of *Busman's Honeymoon*. Simpson played an important part in Mitchell's career, with Anthony Berkeley sponsoring her into the Detection Club in 1933, and introducing her to the fascinations of witchcraft. Mitchell was also "an enthusiastic student of the works of Sigmund Freud" and her other hobbies included "mediaeval architecture and pre-historic sites and exploring those rural settings which add charm and verisimilitude to her books."[3] Her literary interests consisted principally of the works of Ivy Compton-Burnett, P.G. Wodehouse, Damon Runyon and Leonard Q. Ross, "real-life murders and the reminiscences of the great lawyers," and "poetry, mostly

---

1 Blurb published in Penguin edition of Mitchell's books.

2 See: William A.S. Sargeant, "Gladys Mitchell: The Last of the 'Golden Age' Writers," *The Armchair Detective*, Fall 1985, Vol. 18 No. 4.

3 Blurb published in Tom Stacey editions.

the Elizabethans, the Border ballads and the not-quite moderns up to about 1940."[4] She turned her own hand to poetry, producing a single volume titled *The Winnowing*.[5]

In the 1930s and 1940s she was hailed as being at the top of her form. Torquemada of *The Observer* called her "one of the Big Three women detective writers,"[6] the equal of Dorothy L. Sayers and Agatha Christie. Nicholas Blake, reviewing *Dead Men's Morris*, called her "one of the half-dozen best detective writers in this country."[7] *The Times Literary Supplement* named her in "that distinguished group of women authors which includes Miss Dorothy Sayers, Miss Margery Allingham, Mrs. Christie and Miss Ngaio Marsh."[8] Her reputation continued well into the 1960s, when she was described as "another leading lady of English detection scarcely less senior"[9] than Agatha Christie. She was a favourite of many writers. In addition to the adoring Nicholas Blake, her work was admired by Edmund Crispin, Philip Larkin, P. D. James and H.R.F. Keating. Her own opinions of her books are quite interesting. In an interview with Barry Pike in 1976, she named as her favourite books *Laurels are Poison* (1942), which "recalls the college years which I enjoyed so much," *The Rising of the Moon*, "which recalls much of my Brentford childhood," *A Javelin for Jonah* and *Winking at the Brim* (both 1974), and *Convent on Styx* (1975).[10] It is noteworthy that these last three were her most recent titles and hence, perhaps, uppermost in her mind; how else can one explain her fondness for three relatively weak books? Ralph Partridge, who described the celebrated *Dead Men's Morris* as "a towering edifice of inconsequence, pretentiousness, pig-learning and bogus psychology,"[11] was only one of Mitchell's detractors. Rupert Hart-Davis, reviewing *Printer's Error* (1939) in *The Spectator*, believed that "one's expectation of life must be high if one is to pad along ... with Miss Mitchell";[12] and after Blake, *The Spectator* appears to have been allergic to

---

4 Barry Pike, "In Praise of Gladys Mitchell," *The Armchair Detective*, October 1976, Vol. 9 No. 4, p. 252.

5 Date of publication unknown.

6 "Torquemada" (F. Powys Mathers), *The Observer*, 02 October 1938.

7 Nicholas Blake, *The Spectator*, 25 September 1936.

8 *The Times Literary Supplement*, 12 November 1938.

9 *The Times Literary Supplement*, 20 November 1959.

10 Pike, "In Praise," p. 251.

11 Ralph Partridge, *The New Statesman*, 12 September 1936.

12 Rupert Hart-Davis, *The Spectator*, 15 December 1939.

"that tiresome old trout Dame Beatrice Adela Lestrange Bradley,"[13] whose "mannerisms ... [are] the most trying in detective fiction."[14] Mitchell herself confessed that many of her books she was "not exactly proud of, and these are too many to mention," picking out for dis-honourable mention *Printer's Error* and *Brazen Tongue* (1940).[15] In her defence, it must be said that, while *Printer's Error* is too sensational to be entirely convincing, that "horrible book" *Brazen Tongue* must be included among her top three or four stories. It shows the true detective writer's ability to juggle red herrings and to misdirect the reader as much as anything in H.C. Bailey, John Dickson Carr or Christopher Bush.

Of her fellow detective writers, Mitchell particularly admired Sir Arthur Conan Doyle, G. K. Chesterton, H. C. Bailey,[16] Agatha Christie, Ngaio Marsh, Dorothy L. Sayers, Edmund Crispin and Nicholas Blake,[17] Cyril Hare, and, of modern writers, H.R.F. Keating.[18] On the other hand, she disliked the works of Margery Allingham and Michael Innes.[19] Her attitude to the great John Dickson Carr is rather obscure: she confessed to Barry Pike that she "very much like[d] John Dickson Carr as a person, but can't read his books,"[20] yet elsewhere praised "his brilliant and popular books"[21] and "the Chestertonian girth and intellect of Dr. Gideon Fell."[22] Mitchell was the last major detective writer from the 1920s to have continued writing until the 1980s, and was the last member of the Detection Club of the 1930s to survive until that time. Agatha Christie's *Sleeping Murder* was published eight years before *The Crozier Pharaohs*, Mitchell's last novel, and although Margaret Cole and Philip Macdonald died in 1980 and 1981 respectively, their last books had been published in 1942 and 1963.

Mitchell's three greatest gifts, those that set her unmistakably apart from her fellow detective writers, were her imagination, her ability to

---

13 Christopher Pym, *The Spectator*, 01 November 1957.

14 Esther Howard, *The Spectator*, 01 February 1952.

15 Pike, "In Praise," p. 251.

16 Gladys Mitchell, *Sunset Over Soho*, 1988 Sphere Books, p. 73.

17 Pike, "In Praise," p. 252.

18 Gladys Mitchell, "Why Do People Read Detective Stories?" *Murder Ink*, Workman Publishing Co., 1977.

19 Pike, "In Praise," p. 252.

20 Pike, "In Praise," p. 252.

21 Douglas G. Greene, *John Dickson Carr: The Man Who Explained Miracles*. New York: Otto Penzler, 1995, p. 198.

22 Gladys Mitchell, "Why Do People."

create unusual but convincing characters, and her marvelous style; indeed, P.D. James ranked her "among the most felicitous of prose writers."[23] What one looks for in Gladys Mitchell's work is neither Croftsian timetables nor Christiean last-minute surprises, but unorthodoxy: the fantastic, the macabre, the imaginative. Mrs. Bradley is, of course, a witch. She is recognised as such by both Mrs. Fluke of Saxon Wall and Mrs. Harries of Spey, and when dealing with Satanists, she is not averse to frightening secrets out of possible witnesses by drawing crosses in salt. Since she is a witch, it is no wonder that wherever she goes she should find evidence of the supernatural. She finds covens in Norfolk, Wessex and Cornish boarding-houses, and necromancers of all varieties. The ancients believed that every place had a spirit associated with it, and so it is in Mitchell's books, for whether staying with relatives in Oxfordshire or Gloucestershire, investigating a decade-old murder in a house oddly similar to Borley Rectory or staying at a hotel in Winchester, Mrs. Bradley encounters more ghosts than Harry Price. She finds evil wraiths flitting around stone circles, Greek gods inhabiting their ancient shrines, and even the Loch Ness Monster, which devours the murderer at the end of *Winking at the Brim*. In a violation of the rules of the Detection Club, which insists on "a seemly moderation in the use of Ghosts,"[24] supernatural elements are often suggested to be genuine.

The presence of the supernatural adds another level of mystery to Gladys Mitchell's world, and makes it a theatre of war between rationality and superstition. The detective, who usually represents the triumph of law and order over superstition and chaos, is here ambivalent, in possession of occult powers and of a powerful rational scepticism. Even after the criminal mystery has been solved the books remain ambiguous, because the supernatural has not been fully banished. For example, in *Come Away, Death* (1937) and *Wraiths and Changelings* (1978), all the supernatural events are logically explained away— except for one, which leads the *rational* characters, such as Mrs. Bradley and her assistants, to belief in the supernatural. Although that kind of outcome had been suggested in John Dickson Carr's brilliant *The Burning Court* (1937) and H.C. Bailey's "The Profiteers" (1925), these were isolated examples in bodies of work that banished the nightmares of superstition. In

23 *The Times*, 12 March 1981.
24 Greene, *John Dickson Carr*, p. 196.

Mitchell's books, the recurring presence of the supernatural undermines the whole fabric of the rational detective story, and makes of it something unsettling and ambiguous.

When not grappling with the supernatural Mrs. Bradley finds herself grappling with lunatics — often literally, as they try to brain her, drown her or stab her. They are a picturesque lot, these lunatics, from Mrs. Gatty and Mrs. Coutts of Saltmarsh village, to Sir Rudri Hopkinson, who attempts to sacrifice his children, and the psychotic poet T.E. Lawrence (né Swinburne). Fully three-quarters of Mitchell's novels feature madmen, complicated by criminals who frequently counterfeit madness, and the fact that, to the psycho-analyst in Mrs. Bradley, all murderers are mad, because "killing is not a sane reaction to the circumstances of life."[25] So many of the author's characters are deranged in one way or another that the reader is tempted to wonder whether, having caught wind of the eminent psychiatrist's imminent arrival, entire villages decide to go mad to test her powers. Certainly more interesting than being asked to open memorials or fêtes!

One striking feature of Mitchell's work is her choice of setting. One's lasting memories of her novels might sometimes be location — the Scottish Highlands near Glencoe, "reminiscent of the strange and dreadful Mesozoic age, its primordial terrors and grandeurs, its giant-statured vertebrates and all the crude, frightful chaos of pre-history,"[26] and Mitchell's beloved islands, be it the lushness of the aptly named Hombres Muertos or the "bleak, grey, windswept landscape"[27] of Skeleton Island with its lighthouse. (Indeed, the author loves lighthouses. Not only does "A Light on Murder" concern a murder in a lighthouse, the ultimate closed circle with only three possible suspects. One gathers that a similar plot, with a romantic triangle causing bad blood among those forced into such a claustrophobic environment, is also the setting of *Gabriel's Hold*, published in 1935 under the pseudonym of Stephen Hockaby. Against such memorable landscapes, steeped in the history and folklore of the British Isles, and with their towering cliffs, wooded hills, rushing rivers and flowing streams, the author weaves her spellbinding yarns of murder and detection.

---

25 Gladys Mitchell, *The Rising of the Moon*, Virago Press, 1996 p. 125.
26 Gladys Mitchell, *My Father Sleeps*, Severn House, 1981 p. 97.
27 Gladys Mitchell, *Skeleton Island*, Michael Joseph, 1967 p. 10.

It is not only woods and hills that Mitchell uses as setting, but country houses and castles. Although Mrs. Bradley visits Chaynings, Longer House and Merlin's Furlong, the family homes so beloved of Christie and Innes are few and far between in Mitchell's books. Rather it is the establishments of the National Trust (indeed, Timothy Herring, hero of the Malcolm Torrie detective stories, is treasurer of PHISBE, the Society for the Preservation of Buildings of Historic Interest). In addition to Hulliwell Hall, Castle Coldy and Castle Dysey, one of the houses Mrs. Bradley visits in her long career is "Strangers' Hall," which "was built in the early sixteenth century, but on an older foundation. The cellars and part of the ground floor are thirteenth-century and incredibly gloomy, with grained stone ceilings and oddly-shaped nooks and corners."

If Mitchell is fascinated by place, she is equally fond of traveling. Her plots are not static but often involve a great deal of cross-country journeying as Mrs. Bradley hunts up witnesses and suspects, and characters make their pilgrimages. The books are often provided with a detailed itinerary, with descriptions of every town and village visited on the way. At its best it offers the reader an impression of a countryside and a way of life as interesting as the story itself. Whether characters are catching Turkish trains, sailing around the Broads or on a Mediterranean cruise, or on coach tours of Scotland or Wales and Norfolk, Mitchell always provides the detail so beloved of the armchair traveler — and without falling into Freeman Wills Crofts's unfortunate habit of devoting an entire chapter to the workings of the engine. Yet although Mitchell's best tales integrate setting and detection, many of her late books over-emphasise setting, relegating the plot to a back burner. *Adders on the Heath* (1963), for example, epitomises all of the author's flaws.

Mitchell's plotting style was uniquely hers. In addition to populating her stories with uncanny elements, she wove some of the most divertingly complex murder mysteries, plots fuelled by identical twins, mistaken identity, impersonation, lunacy (whether real or assumed), secret love affairs and all the traditional ingredients of the comedy of errors until the plot thickened like a stew. Complexity fascinated her, necessitating in the earlier books chapters of Mrs. Bradley's notes and "End Papers." Yet so skillfully were her skeins unraveled, so delicately did she reveal the subsidiary mysteries in each chapter — and, in several instances, the murderer midway through the book — that the alert reader (and readers very soon learnt to be alert!) felt himself in full possession of the facts. Although adept at constructing complicated murder mazes where every fact fitted at the end, occasionally her maze-building would get out of hand, and she would lose herself in the labyrinth, whereupon the critical Minotaur would gobble her up, and, like Icarus, she would come plummeting down to earth a fantastic wreck. This is particularly damaging in *Here Comes a Chopper* (1946), a book that keeps the reader captivated with humour, action and characterisation until the end, when the whole thing suddenly falls apart. In the final chapters characters start behaving in ways unknown to god, man or beast, rushing around and either shooting or being shot at, while others try to conceal misdemeanours the reader had not known of until that page. The grand confrontation between two women, both lovers of the victim, bears little relation to any other event in the book. The result: it is impossible to spot the murderer's accomplice, despite the cryptic utterances of Mrs. Bradley. Even worse is the fact that the identity of the murderer proper is clever, with plenty of good clues to back it up. When one considers that Mitchell's books are full of odd and diverting incident, complication piled upon complication in a giddying tower, and the thousand and one details of good food and scenic countryside, the resulting dish is perhaps too rich for some tastes. At such times even the most indulgent reader comes to the conclusion that, like the events of *The Tempest*,

> *This is as strange a maze as e'er men trod*
> *And there is in this business more than nature*
> *Was ever conduct of: some oracle*
> *Must rectify our knowledge.*

Invariably that oracle is Mrs. Bradley, in fiction a direct descendant of Prospero. She has superhuman, indeed supernatural, status, conversing with spirits and Classical gods alike, conjuring up occult powers to do her bidding and working much magic to further the web of her design. Every strand of the plot is as firmly in her hands as in those of the Fates. She decides the destinies of good and wicked alike, benignly and serenely, detecting and punishing conspiracies and attempts on her life, bringing young lovers together, minor criminals to repentance and murderers to the gallows, even personally orchestrating their demises.

Beatrice Adela Lestrange Bradley, consulting psychiatrist to the Home Office, is one of the most memorable detectives in fiction, ranking with Dr. Fell, Sir Henry Merrivale, Hercule Poirot, Father Brown and Joshua Clunk. She was described by Torquemada as "by far the best and most vital English female detective; indeed, as far as I am concerned, she is the only one."[28] Where Christie's Miss Marple relies on knitting and gossip to solve her cases, Mrs. Bradley has no time for such an approach, for she is no sweet old woman. On her first appearance, in *Speedy Death*, where she commits the second murder, Alastair Bing is reminded

> of the reconstruction of a pterodactyl he had once seen in a German museum. There was the same inhuman malignity in her expression as in that of the defunct bird, and, like it, she had a cynical smirk about her mouth even when in repose. She possessed nasty, dry, claw-like hands, and her arms, yellow and curiously repulsive, suggested the plucked wings of a fowl...[29]
> Strange to say, her voice belied her appearance, for, instead of the birdlike twitter one might have expected to hear issuing from those beaked lips, her utterance was slow, mellifluous, and slightly drawled; unctuous, rich, and reminiscent of dark, smooth treacle.[30]

She is always described in reptilian terms. In *Dead Men's Morris*, she has "the maternal anxiety of a boa-constrictor which watches its young attempting to devour their first donkey."[31] (Mitchell's metaphors are often as startling as the incidents in her books!) She is physically and mentally alert: she drops from windows to the street below, "she was ... the most brilliant darts player and knife thrower that I have ever seen ... [and] a dead shot with an airgun,"[32] and she can break a man's wrist with ease. Attempts on her life — made, among others, by a murderous Robin Hood who attempts to transfix her to a tree with an arrow, by a professional wife-drowner who hopes to secure her fortune, and by a nest of Satanists in Norfolk who shoot venom-tipped darts at her from a passing car — are often met with a hideous screech of laughter.

Her light reading consists of modern poetry, and, when in Greece, history and mythology, turning *The Iliad* to both detection and the

---

28 "Torquemada" (F. Powys Mathers): *The Observer*, 28 July 1935.
29 Gladys Mitchell, *Speedy Death*, Hogarth Press, 1988 p. 11.
30 Gladys Mitchell, *Speedy Death*, p. 13.
31 Gladys Mitchell, *Dead Men's Morris*, Michael Joseph, 1986 p. 147.
32 Gladys Mitchell, *The Saltmarsh Murders*, Hogarth Press, 1984 p. 48.

prevention of human sacrifice. Imperturbable, utterly cynical, and omniscient, the only thing she does not know is

> exactly what went on in the Cities of the Plain. Even allowing for all the sources and idiosyncrasies of human behaviour which modern psychology has laid bare, it is difficult to conceive of a state of things so far removed from normal conduct that the cities had to be destroyed in so uncompromising a fashion. One thinks of post-1918 Hamburg; one thinks of the port of Suez; one thinks unutterable thoughts; and, after that, imagination boggles, as the master of the comic novel has said.[33]

Her morality is entirely her own, for she recognises that every human being is a potential murderer, "some in deed and some in thought," the only difference being that "some have the courage of their convictions" while "others have not."[34] She views murder, on occasions, as a necessary step. It is also clear that her creator, progressive even by our standards, used Mrs. Bradley as a mouthpiece for her controversial views on such taboo subjects as adultery, the death sentence, life imprisonment and the treatment of the insane. Although in every respect a modern emancipated woman, Mrs. Bradley is linked to the past: an ancestress, Mary Toadflax, was tried in Scotland for witchcraft in the time of James I,

> but was let off by the favour of the presiding magistrate, whose paramour she was said to be when the devil was occupied elsewhere and her incubus not in the mood.[35]

After the curious mixture of poltergeists, practical jokes, skeletons, cauldrons, vipers and drowned cooks that is *Laurels are Poison*, Mrs. Bradley recruited as secretary the galumphing Laura Catriona Menzies (later Gavin, married to a policeman she encounters in the 1947 novel *Death and the Maiden*), with an endless enthusiasm for everything, particularly her native Scotland and tracking desperadoes across the British landscape. This is perhaps the best Holmes / Watson pairing since the original. In some novels, such as *Twelve Horses and the Hangman's*

---

33 Gladys Mitchell, *Watson's Choice*, Michael Joseph, 1985 p. 142.

34 Gladys Mitchell, *Speedy Death*, p. 67.

35 Gladys Mitchell, *Death and the Maiden*, Michael Joseph, 1947 p. 172.

Noose (1956) and *Skeleton Island* (1967), Laura takes centre stage, much to the reader's alarm and dismay. She is highly effective when, as in Kipling, her head is sat on till the morning. When Mrs. Bradley is toned down — in fact, no longer Mrs. Bradley but Dame Beatrice by this time — and Laura exaggerated, one agrees with Edmund Crispin's statement that

> there are other readers who like myself wish that Laura had been impaled by a javelin before she ever had a chance to settle in at Wandles Parva; but it is only fair to Miss Mitchell to say that some have liked the girl very much indeed.[36]

The Works

The earliest books from the period 1929–1955 are light-hearted parodies of the conventions of the genre, with the movements of the suspects intricately worked out, in some cases to five minutes. There is brilliant clueing (the 1930 novel *The Longer Bodies*, in particular, has a wonderful clue in the form of a hideous statue and a game of darts) and a complex but easily understood plot. *The Mystery of a Butcher's Shop* (1929), which followed *Speedy Death*, is set in a small English village similar to Christie's St. Mary Mead, complete with absent-minded vicar, philandering doctor, dissolute young artists and an unpopular squire who, as the title suggests, is cut into sausages and hung from hooks in the butcher's lock-up shop. The solution is a staggering surprise. *The Saltmarsh Murders* (1932), one of her best-known titles, turns Christie's *The Murder at the Vicarage* (1930) on its head, with its vicar, vicar's wife, curate (who, of course, narrates in a Wodehousian manner) and assorted lunatics at the centre of the tale. *Death at the Opera* was published in 1934, the year that Ngaio Marsh's first novel, *A Man Lay Dead*, appeared. With its amateur theatrical setting (a school production of *The Mikado*) and emphasis on the movement of the actors on and offstage, it is very Marshy indeed. The motive is highly original, and the scenes with a devotee of George Joseph Smith are wonderfully amusing.

The publication of *The Devil at Saxon Wall* in 1935 marked a new period in Mitchell's writing, with an emphasis on the supernatural, on folklore, and on history. These tales are much longer than their pre–

---

36 Edmund Crispin, "Durable Dame," *The Sunday Times*, 07 March 1976.

decessors. While the plots are more complex, the structure of the stories is far less reliant on that of the orthodox detective story, and far closer to that of the pure novel. Instead of a mathematical study of the killing committed in the library between the hours of seven and ten, with serial interviewing of suspects and an odd murder here and there, Mitchell builds up pictures of a larger world. Here are the good things of life, hearty Christmas dinners and convivial family gatherings, the pleasures of travelling throughout the Mediterranean, along with the busyness of conventual life, or a small town coping with the onset of the Second World War. The small details of nature and place build up the picture of a world fully imagined, a world as tangible in every respect as the world in which we move. To give herself more leisure to weave a richly detailed tapestry, Mitchell devises new ways of treating the murderous problem, often delaying the murder, as in *Come Away, Death* (1937), until late in the book. The plotting is non-linear. Thus, although her plots are logically and soundly constructed, various events and their significance are revealed later, in a piece-meal way, so that the reader is forced to be alert in order to piece together the strands of the tangled web Mitchell weaves. This applies particularly to *Dead Men's Morris* and *Brazen Tongue.*

After 1942, when Laura Menzies was introduced, many of the books in that decade were adventure stories, set against well-evoked landscapes (although Edmund Crispin complained of her habit of "verbalising maps") as Mrs. Bradley confronts Satanists on the Norfolk Broads in *The Worsted Viper* (1943), criminal gangs on the Highland moors in *Hangman's Curfew* (1941) and *My Father Sleeps* (1944) and, in the best of these thrillers, an art-smuggling ring with hidden connections to the circle of standing stones known as *The Dancing Druids* (1948). Later stories, such as *Faintley Speaking* (1954) and *Skeleton Island,* would also make use of the thriller form but to less effect. This decade also boasts some of Mitchell's most interesting works. *Sunset Over Soho* (1943) is a fascinating but flawed tale of the London underworld which draws in boating on England's waterways, adultery, sinister Spaniards, and a corpse in a makeshift coffin turned up by enemy action. It suffers from an extraordinary degree of complexity and narrative hopscotch worthy of Tristram Shandy. *The Rising of the Moon* (1945), the author's most popular book, a mixture of Dickens and the Brothers Grimm, is the story of two orphans (based on the author and her brother) who attempt to track down a "Ripper" in Brentford, where Mitchell lived as a child. It has autobiographical elements to which she would return in *Late, Late in the Evening* (1976) and *The Greenstone Griffins* (1983). *Death and the Maiden*, one of the author's greatest triumphs, achieves the greatest possible complexity but uses only four suspects and two corpses — two local boys apparently drowned by a naiad, an idea only Mitchell could pull off successfully. As the Hughesian title suggests, *Tom Brown's Body* (1949) returns to the school setting of *Death at the Opera*, this time with witchcraft added for zest and Mrs. Bradley conjuring up visions for the blind witch Lecky Harries at the end. But though highly entertaining, the revelation of the murderer is a disappointment.

The books of the early 1950s continued the heady mixture of detection and supernatural elements, with Mrs. Bradley somewhat toned down but still gloriously reptilian. Although Laura Menzies is largely or entirely absent from many of these tales, the supernatural or the untoward are ever-present, appearing in the form of a ghost in rural Gloucestershire (*Groaning Spinney*), a sinister pair of identical and androgynous twins and Sir Adrian Caux, their "maniacal and homicidal grandfather who cheats at country-house cricket" (*The Echoing Strangers*, 1952), and a coven under the supervision of a necromantic don straight out of M.R. James (*Merlin's Furlong*, 1953).

The murder of Mrs. Bradley at the hands of Dame Beatrice in 1956 marks a decline in the quality of Mitchell's books — but she had, after all, been writing for nigh on 30 years. In many books of the late 1950s and 1960s (such as *Adders on the Heath*, 1963, and *Death of a Delft Blue*, 1964) imagination has given way to routine. Dame Beatrice is a shadow of her former self, the bony claw tucked quietly away in her knitting, the horrible leer wiped off her face, the eldritch cackle silenced. Rather than terrifying her suspects into betraying themselves before, in certain cases, usurping the public hangman's duty, here it is not the criminal but reader whom she kills — boring him to death without her auger-sharp wit in evidence. Laura Gavin, too, has become intolerable with her hyper-activity. It is disheartening to find oneself cheering for the opposing side. Such things are, after all, not cricket, whatever Sir Adrian Caux may think. Although the evocation of landscape had always been an admirable Mitchell trait, in the later books setting obviously came before plot. There is a loss of ingenuity, and the reader who witnesses Mitchell's Herculean but ultimately pointless attempts to accommodate large swathes of English countryside in a 190-page detective story can only feel disappointment. Thus *Adders on the Heath* (1963), Mitchell's nadir as writer and as detective novelist, opens with the intriguing situation of a man finding a dead body in his tent; when he returns with the police, the body has been exchanged for another. Yet this simple circumstance takes several chapters to accomplish. Why the obvious yet characterless murderers should have bothered to exchange the corpses is never made clear, for they certainly derive no benefit from it. Another weakness is the preposterous idea that smugglers (or are they Communists?) should communicate by transmitting secret codes via Hampshire ponies. Yet if the works overall became more uneven, books of this quality are, thankfully, few and far between. The enjoyably imaginative stories from this period include *The Croaking Raven* (1966), in which Dame Beatrice and co. hire a Norman castle for the holidays only to find themselves involved in a complicated tale of inheritances, ghosts and missing heirs; and *Dance to Your Daddy* (1969), a delightful parody of the Gothic romance, complete with sinister scheming guardian and hapless maiden.

Many of the works of the 1970s and 1980s, the final two decades of Mitchell's life and writing career, are similarly uneven. The average work of this time concerns a tour group of some variety traipsing around Britain or Greece, visiting sites of interest before one of their number is murdered. Most frequently this is a middle-aged termagant, killed by one whose identity, when revealed, is often anti-climactic (or would be, if there were more tension). The minutiae of travelling, including descriptions of every way-stop, is laboriously detailed. But again, some novels are recommendable. *The Whispering Knights* (1980), concerning stone circles, is quite entertaining, and one can single out a number of titles that do not resort to formula: *Nest of Vipers* (1979), concerning a coven of witches that has established itself in a Cornish boarding-house; *Here Lies Gloria Mundy* (1982), in which the titular character is murdered and rises from the dead; and, above all, the superb *Greenstone Griffins*, the last book published in Mitchell's lifetime (although three more appeared after her death), which combines the historiographical investigation of *When Last I Died* (1941) with the autobiographical elements of *The Rising of the Moon* in an entirely novel manner.

The world of Gladys Mitchell is an extraordinary place, one where the plots have "all the mad logic of a dream," where the detective is alternately sorceress and psychoanalyst, where the murderer is just as likely to be devoured by Nessie as more prosaically arrested, where half the characters are mad and the other half "as mad as Hamlet," where every man lives by a churchyard and the supernatural lingers on, and where the mood is "tragedy, comedy, history, pastoral, pastoral-comical, historical-pastoral, tragical-historical, tragical-comical-historical-pastoral." Let the reader of these stories enter this brave new world with joy and awe, and then plunge into the sixty-six novels which feature Mrs. Bradley. I envy them their first encounters with the most extraordinary mind of the detective story, one in whose hands the detective story "suffer[ed] a sea change into something rich and strange." And how better than through *Sleuth's Alchemy*?

— Nicholas Fuller.

The Case of the Hundred Cats

From the very first I myself suspected the aunt. We had been asked to see a patient who suffered from periodic loss of memory, but Mrs. Bradley — who was carrying out a delicate Home Office job at the time — was not prepared to undertake the case, so I thought I would ring up John.

"Is that the house where they keep all those cats?" he asked.

"I don't know, John."

"Well, it is. That woman takes drugs."

"You won't accept the case, then?"

"No, I won't. They called me in last month, and I told them then what I thought. Mrs. What's-it is trying to get the other one's money. She'll get her certified if she possibly can."

I wrote to Mrs. Dudley, the woman who had sent me the letter, and told her to bring the patient to see me.

The two of them came next day, a woman of fifty or so, in very somber clothes, with a heavy face purple with powder and too much eye shadow on, and a frail, anemic-looking younger woman who seemed too timid even to give her name.

Ethel let them in to the consulting room, and I sat behind the largest of the three desks, fountain pen in hand, and horn-rimmed goggles on nose, and tried not to look like the prettiest secretary in London.

"Mrs. and Miss Dudley?" I asked, making rapid hieroglyphics on a pad.

"Mrs. and Miss Dudley. Yes, that's right," the elderly lady said.

"Then, may I see Miss Dudley alone?"

"No, no!" said the girl, in a whining voice. "I had really rather you didn't!"

"You see, I'm afraid you're not quite clear — " said the aunt. I looked from one to the other.

"It is customary for the patients themselves to describe to me their symptoms. In this way I can tell whether the case is of sufficient importance for Mrs. Bradley to handle," I said with exceptional rudeness. I disliked Mrs. Dudley at sight, and as for the niece, I never saw any one who made me feel more irritable. "Then do I understand — oh, then you are not Mrs. Bradley?" the elder lady said.

"I'm the secretary. It is my duty to keep Mrs. Bradley's engagement book up to date. If I think there is no case of sufficient importance for her I send the patients elsewhere — to Sir John MacGovern, for example. But, of course, I can't tell anything about the case until I have questioned the patient alone," I added, turning to the younger woman again.

I saw them look at each other — just a flash, but unmistakable when you're looking out for such a response. The elder woman cleared her throat a little. People often dislike me — I am too pretty and too efficient, I suppose. The first antagonises women, the second men. It is unfortunate for me, in a way.

The elder woman rose.

"Very well. I suppose you mean you want to question us separately. Where shall I wait?"

I rang for Ethel to show her into the lounge. It was eleven o'clock. Ethel, I knew, would settle her down in the lounge and bring her sweet biscuits and coffee, and perhaps a Turkish cigarette, thus producing, as exactly as possible, the psychological effects of the lounge of one of the big London stores, where women of this type seem to spend their time. Besides, these would keep her occupied whilst I questioned the patient, and, even if she wondered all the time what was being asked and answered, experience had informed us that her wondering would be of a comparatively charitable kind.

As soon as she had gone I settled down to it.

"Do you want to come to Mrs. Bradley for some treatment?" I enquired. The patient looked at me with her large, weak, silly, blue eyes, and nodded.

"Is that the truth? Or did your aunt bring you here against your will?" I said. It was a pretty direct suggestion, but she ignored it.

"I wanted to come. I am very ill. I think I am going to die," the poor foolish creature observed, in the same thin, wailing voice as she had used when her aunt was in the room.

"You take drugs, don't you?" I said, remembering what John had told me over the telephone.

"Sometimes. When the cats get very bad."

"The cats?"

"I do love them. They are dears. But they scratch me sometimes. Look!" She glanced fearfully round at the door, then showed me her neck and shoulder, pulling the blouse away with such nervous fingers that one of the buttons flew off.

"I must sew that on before auntie sees it," she said.

We both went down on our knees in search of it, and when it was found she stuffed it into the pocket of her suit, beneath a handkerchief.

"I'm scratched all over," she said.

"But all these scratches are dangerous! How many cats have you got?"

"A hundred, and I love them all," she said. The bending about had brought colour into her cheeks, and she looked a good deal prettier.

"A hundred?" I said. "And when you lose your memory, do you forget the cats?"

"No, never. I always remember the cats. At least, the cats are the last things I think about when I lose my memory, and the first things I think about when it comes back to me."

Do you wander away from your home?"

"Oh, yes. They find me usually at the Zoo."

"At the Zoo? What makes you go there?"

"I haven't the slightest idea. I'm always looking at birds when I go to the Zoo. I believe I think I'm a cat."

She was gaining much more confidence. She was leaning forward a little, absorbed in what she was saying. "You see," she added, "I really live two lives."

"Most people live more than two lives. They live six or seven," I assured her.

At Adelheim, where I was trained, they always insisted that we must adopt a brisk and businesslike cheerfulness with the patients.

But this patient, who had begun to creep out of her shell, instantly drew back again, and, for a bit, would not answer my questions at all, except with a nervous laugh.

"What do you want Mrs. Bradley to do? Do you know?" I demanded.

"I only want her to write a certificate, and send a copy of it to my banker, to say I am perfectly sane," the poor girl replied, with a sudden return to composure which took my breath away.

"But who on earth thinks you are anything else?" I said, as though in great surprise. As a matter of fact, most of these under-developed, hysterical subjects *do* think that some one believes them to be insane.

She shrugged. Then she got up abruptly.

"You'll ask her to see me, won't you? Before I lose my memory again? Mrs. Bradley, I mean. You'll get her to see me, won't you? When auntie isn't there. Like this. Like this."

"I'll ask her," I answered. (Whether she'll come is another matter, I thought.) "Yes, I'll certainly ask her. Do you know — have you any idea — what brings on these lapses of memory? Does your aunt — do you quarrel at all?"

"Quarrel? One doesn't — quarrel with grown-up people."

I was annoyed.

"How old are you then, Miss Dudley?"

"Miss Dudley! How funny that sounds? They always call me Lily. That's what you'll put on the certificate for me, won't you? Lily Dudley is sane."

She went out, looking at me over her shoulder with those great, pale, silly, blue eyes.

I telephoned Mrs. Bradley, and she told me to call at her Kensington house and have tea. She was fairly late getting in, so we made it dinner, instead, and I wore my new pansy-black. Mrs. Bradley eyed it approvingly.

"And what supreme idiocy have you committed this time, child?" said she.

I told her about the case. She grinned, looking just like an alligator.

"I must attend another sitting of this Lunacy Laws Commission thing to-morrow, but on Thursday I could see these Dudleys," she said. "Make the appointment for three in the afternoon, at their private house. I like to know the environment of these loss of memory cases. And I want to see the letter. You have it, haven't you, child?"

I took it out of my handbag, and passed it across the table.

"Aha!" said Mrs. Bradley. In her sea-green dinner gown and with her yellow skin, she looked like a smiling snake. I watched her, fascinated, as she took the letter in her skinny claw and with horrible cackles read it.

"Treasure it, child," she said. "You had better come with me on Thursday. Now go and ring up our friend, Inspector Toogarde, and tell him to keep a watch on the house. If he can find any manner or means of excuse, he's to see that the young woman is arrested. The sooner that's done, the better."

"The *young* woman? Oh — to keep her safe from the aunt!" We had never before employed protective arrest in a case, but I had heard of it.

"To keep her safe from the aunt," said Mrs. Bradley. She cackled wildly. She took me to the theatre after dinner and we picked up John in the vestibule.

"What's this about these cats?" asked Mrs. Bradley.

"Cats?" said John. "Oh, did Nancy tell you? Cats. Oh, yes." He stampeded us into our stalls and then studied the programme. Mrs. Bradley gave him a dig in the ribs.

"And you'd better write to Mrs. Dudley, and tell her my fee is payable in advance," she said to me.

"Very well, if you wish it," I said.

"I'm listening," John remarked, caressing his lower ribs.

"Tell me about the cats, child. The curtain goes up, or should do, in ten minutes' time."

"Well, just that they keep cats, you know. The whole place swarms with cats. And the stink! Phew! Awful! And yet, a funny thing." He paused; a habit he has.

"Go on!" we said together.

"Mixed with this awful catty stench, which pervades the whole of the house, there was a faint odour of sanctity, so to speak, which seemed just vaguely familiar," said John, caressing his chin.

"Proceed," said Mrs. Bradley.

"Oh, I don't know. I could have placed it but for the all-pervasive stench of those beastly cats. I connect it with that American show we visited last year. You know the place I mean."

Mrs. Bradley's eyes were snapping.

"Go on, child, do," she said.

"I can't. Don't know any more. I knew the woman was taking drugs. I said so. Gave her to understand I'd put the police on her track."

"And what stuff do you think it was? Cocaine?" I demanded, abruptly. We had never had a dope-fiend on our books.

John laughed.

"It wasn't cocaine."

"What do you know about poisons, John?" asked Mrs. Bradley, suddenly.

"Nothing, beyond what all alienists learn in a routine way for rapid diagnosis or morbid symptoms, of course."

"Interesting," said Mrs. Bradley absently. "I wish I could cut that conference tomorrow. But I can't. I'm down to speak. Let me beg of you, child," she said to me, "on no account to go round to that house alone."

I promised, and the curtain went up just then. During the intervals Mrs. Bradley would not discuss the case, but bought us pink gins and made weird hieroglyphics all over her programme while we stood in the bar and drank them.

"Keep me in touch with any developments, child," she said that night, before we parted. John took me out to supper. It was an extension night. We danced a good deal, and I was so tired that Ethel had to wake me in the morning.

"I brought your early tea, miss, nearly an hour ago, but you was off that sound!" she said. "So now I've brought your breakfast, and here's the letters, miss."

So I breakfasted in bed, and read Mrs. Dudley's second letter. They were going away to Broadstairs, it announced, and if I would write the certificate which had been asked for — they understood from the medical directory that I was entirely qualified to do this — they need not trouble us further. The letter bore the postmark of ten p.m., and was headed, "Nine forty-five."

I rang up Mrs. Bradley at her house. The conference began at eleven, so I knew she would still be at home.

"Telephone Inspector Toogarde and tell him to watch the house. I *wish* he'd arrest the niece, tell him," said Mrs. Bradley.

Next day I called for her and we both went round to what Americans would call the Dudley residence. It was an old house with a basement.

"Well, any developments, Albert?" asked Mrs. Bradley, for the inspector had put a man outside the door.

"No, ma'am." He saluted.

"Not even a light in the basement?" asked Mrs. Bradley. The constable looked puzzled.

"Yes. There *was* a light in the basement. I never thought anything of it. There wasn't no noise," he observed.

"Oh, wasn't there?" said Mrs. Bradley briskly. "When your officer comes along, you'd better tell him to go down and dig for the body."

She went up to the door and knocked. There was silence. Then there came the sound of footsteps, and, at the same time, a kind of rushing noise. Mrs. Bradley pulled me aside so that both of us were pressed against the coping at the top of the short flight of steps.

"Lean back as far as you can. Here come the cats," she said.

As soon as the door was opened, out they came — Siamese, Persian, tabby, Manx, males and females — one animal, I am certain, was a lynx, and I'm sure I saw a Scottish wildcat, but they all shot past so quickly that it was impossible almost to see them. Then a whining voice said sadly:

"Oh, dear! That's all auntie's cats."

"*Your* cats, you mean," said Mrs. Bradley sharply. She put out a yellow claw, seized the woman by the wrist and stared down at the writhing fingers.

"Albert, child, do you want your promotion?" she called. The prisoner bent her head towards Mrs. Bradley's wrist.

"Not 'arf ma'am, please," said the policeman grinning. He swung up the steps and grabbed Mrs. Bradley's captive, who was fighting and clawing, more like a cat herself than a human being.

"Quiet, will you?" demanded the constable. The prisoner began to cry. "And what shall I charge her with, ma'am? — assault and battery, or is it an R.S.P.C.A. case with all them cats?"

"Charge her with murder, and see how she likes it," said Mrs. Bradley brutally. And sure enough, it was not much later that she and John were watching Inspector Toogarde taking the body up from under the basement floor. Mrs. Bradley sighed when she saw me again.

"It's a pity I had that conference yesterday. Still, Toogarde has got his prisoner, and I expect that's all he'll care."

"But did that spineless creature *really* murder her aunt?" I could not believe it possible.

Mrs. Bradley looked at her yellow wrist where teeth-marks were plainly visible. She did not answer the question. There was no need.

"There were one or two interesting points about the story you told me," she said, "although I don't think you noticed. The first thing that struck me was that evidently you had taken it for granted that the older woman must be the married woman. This was not necessarily true. Then came the extraordinary contrast between the way the younger woman spoke when something important was on hand, and her remarks when the matter under discussion was not germane to her purpose."

"Oh? Do you mean the lucid way she told me her aunt was going to get her certified, and wanted me to testify she was sane?" I began to see the point of that interview now.

"It was when you told me she wanted you to send a copy of the certificate to her banker, that I became so extremely suspicious," said Mrs. Bradley. "It so happens that one of the most unpleasant experiences of my life was when I helped to certify a perfectly sane man on the evidence of relatives who wanted to administer his estate. Luckily, we put that right in time, but since then, as soon as I hear lunacy and bankers mentioned together, all my suspicions are aroused. In this particular case, for instance, if Miss Dudley were, the older woman and Mrs. Dudley the younger, why didn't the younger one undeceive you?"

"Well, why didn't the older one? It was equally apparent to her."

"I fancy, if you refer to your notes of the conversation, that she did attempt to put you right on the point, but that you yourself interrupted her, and then you sent her away. Well, the whole thing sounded, to my possibly morbid mind, just sufficiently extraordinary to warrant my interference. But I think the affair was well on its way by the time they came to you here. Of course, it was the aunt who took drugs, I knew that from your description of her face. It was the niece who procured enough of the valerian for murder."

"Valerian?"

"Cats," said Mrs. Bradley succinctly. "It was when John mentioned the cats and their smell and then the other smell which he almost thought he could recognise, that I began to smell, not a rat, but a murder. You see, in that American hospital he mentioned, they gave the patients small doses of valerian as a sedative. They stain the stuff pink there, and slightly flavour it with essence of clove. It was the clove, I dare say, that he smelt."

"But I still don't understand about the certificate."

"*Miss* Dudley, the older lady, the aunt by marriage, had made a will in niece *Mrs.* Dudley's favour. The latter wanted *Miss* Dudley — *Lily* Dudley — certified sane, so that, *whatever* happened later, the will remained valid and no other relatives could plead unsound mind in the testatrix, because of our medical and psychoanalytical evidence."

"But how do you *know* that the young one was Mrs. Dudley? The thing seems to turn upon that."

"When I grasped her hand at the door, I looked for the mark of the wedding ring, child. It was there."

Daisy Bell

Daisy, Daisy, give me your answer, do!
I've gone crazy, all for the love of you!
It won't be a stylish marriage — We can't afford a carriage — But you'll look neat upon the seat
Of a bicycle made for two.

In the curved arm of the bay the sea lay perfectly still. Towards the horizon was reflected back the flashing light of the sun, but under the shadow of huge cliffs the dark-green water was as quiet as a lake at evening.

Above, riding over a ridge between two small villages, went the road, a dusty highway once, a turnpike on which the coach had changed horses three times in twenty miles. That dusty road was within the memory of the villagers; in the post office there were picture postcards, not of the coaches, certainly, but of the horse-drawn station bus on the shocking gradients and hairpin bends of the highway.

The road was now slightly wider — not much, because every extra foot had to be hacked from the rocky hillside, for on one side the road fell almost sheer to the sea. A humped turf edge kept this seaward boundary (insufficiently, some said, for there had been motoring accidents, especially in the dark), and beyond the humped edge, and, treacherously, just out of sight of motorists who could see the rolling turf but not the danger, there fell away a Gadarene descent of thirteen hundred feet.

George took the road respectfully, with an eye for hairpin bends and (although he found this irksome) an occasional toot on the horn. His employer, small, spare, and upright, sat beside him, the better to admire the rolling view. Equally with the moorland scenery she admired her chauffeur's driving. She was accustomed to both phenomena, but neither palled on her. In sixteen crawling miles she had not had a word to say.

At the County Boundary, however, she turned her head slightly to the right.

"The next turning, George. It's narrow."

His eyes on the road ahead, the chauffeur nodded, and the car turned off to the left down a sandy lane, at the bottleneck of which it drew up courteously in face of a flock of lively, athletic, headstrong moorland sheep. The shepherd saluted Mrs. Bradley, passed the time of day with the chauffeur, said it was a pity all they motors shouldn't have the same danged sense, and urged his charges past the car, and kept them within some sort of bounds with the help of a shaggy dog.

At the bottom of the slope, and wedged it seemed in the hollow, was a village with a very small church. Mrs. Bradley went into the churchyard to inspect the grave of an ancestress (she believed) of her own who had died in the odour of sanctity, but, if rumour did not lie, only barely so, for she had enjoyed a reputation as a witch.

Mrs. Bradley, looking (with her black hair, sharp black eyes, thin hands, and beaky little mouth) herself not at all unlike a witch, spent an interesting twenty minutes or so in the churchyard, and then went into the church.

Its architectural features were almost negligible. A fourteenth-century chancel (probably built on the site of the earliest church), a badly restored nave, a good rood screen, and the only remaining bit of Early English work mutilated to allow for an organ loft, were all obvious. There seemed, in fact, very little, on a preliminary investigation, to interest even the most persistent or erudite visitor.

In the dark south wall, however, of what had been the Lady Chapel, Mrs. Bradley came upon a fourteenth-century piscina whose bowl had been carved in the likeness of a hideous human head. She took out a magnifying glass and examined the carving closely. Montague Rhodes James, with his genius for evoking unquiet imaginings and terrifying, atavistic fears, might have described the expression upon its horrid countenance. All that Mrs. Bradley could accomplish was a heathenish muttering indicative of the fact that, in her view, the countenance betrayed indication of at least two major Freudian complexes and a Havelock Ellis regression into infantile criminology.

"A murderer's face, ma'am," said a voice behind her. "Ay, as I stand, that be a murderer's face."

She turned and saw the verger with his keys. "Ay, they do tell, and vicar he do believe it, as carver was vouchsafed a true, just vision of Judas Iscariot the traitor, and carved he out for all to look upon."

He smiled at her almost with the sinister leer of the carving itself, thought Mrs. Bradley, startled by the change in his mild and previously friendly expression. He passed on into the vestry, dangling his keys.

Shaking her head, Mrs. Bradley dropped some money into the offertory box on the pillar nearest the porch, and took the long sloping path between the headstones of the graves to the lych-gate. Here she found George in conversation with a black-haired woman. George had always given himself (with how much truth his employer had never troubled herself to find out) the reputation of being a misogynist, and on this occasion, seated on the step of the car, he was, in his own phrase, "laying down the law" with scornful masculine firmness. The girl had her back to the lych-gate. She was plump and bareheaded, and was wearing brown corduroy shorts, a slightly rucked-up blouse on elastic at the waist, and — visible from the back view which Mrs. Bradley had of her — a very bright pink vest which showed between the trucked-up blouse and the shorts. For the rest she was brown-skinned and, seen face to face, rather pretty.

A tandem bicycle, built to accommodate two men, was resting against the high, steep, ivy-grown bank of the lane. The young woman, seeing Mrs. Bradley, who had in fact strolled round to get a view of her, cut short George's jeremiads by thanking him. Then she walked across the road, set the tandem upright, pushed it sharply forward, and, in spite of the fact that the slope of the road was against her, mounted with agility and ease on to the front saddle. Then she tacked doggedly up the hill, the tandem, lacking any weight on the back seat, wagging its tail in what looked to Mrs. Bradley a highly dangerous manner as it zigzagged up to the bend in the lane and wobbled unwillingly round it.

George had risen to his feet upon the approach of his employer, and now stood holding the door open.

"A courageous young woman, George?" suggested Mrs. Bradley, getting into the car.

"A foolish one, madam, in my opinion," George responded primly, "and so I was saying to her when she was asking the way. Looking for trouble I call it to cycle one of them things down these roads. Look at the hill she's coming to, going to Lyndale this route. Meeting her husband, she says; only been married a month, and having their honeymoon now and using the tandem between them; him having to work thereabouts, and her cycling that contraption down from London, where she's living with her mother while he gets the home for her.

Taken three days to do it in, and meeting him on top of Lyndale Hill this afternoon. More like a suicide pact, if you ask me what I think."

"I not only ask you, George, but I am so much enthralled by what you think that I propose we take the same route and follow her."

"We were due to do so in any case, madam, if I can find a place to turn the car in this lane."

It took him six slow miles to find a suitable place. During the drive towards the sea, the big car brushing the summer hedgerows almost all the time, Mrs. Bradley observed,

"I don't like to think of that young woman, George. I hope you advised her to wheel the bicycle on all dangerous parts of the road?"

"As well advise an errand boy to fit new brake-blocks, madam," George austerely answered. "I did advise her to that effect, but not to cut any ice. She fancies herself on that jigger. You can't advise women of that age."

"Did you offer her any alternative route to Lyndale?"

"Yes, madam; not with success."

At the top of the winding hill he turned to the left, and then, at the end of another five miles and a quarter of wind and the screaming seabirds, great stretches of moorland heather, bright green tracks of little peaty streams, and, south of the moor, the far-off ridges and tors, he engaged his lowest gear again and the car crept carefully down a long, steep, dangerous hill. There were warning notices on either side of the road, and the local authority, laying special emphasis on the subject of faulty brakes, had cut a parking space from the edge of the stubborn moor. The gradient of the steepest part of the hill was one in four. The car took the slant like a cat in sight of a bird.

"What do you think of our brakes, George?" Mrs. Bradley inquired. George replied, in the reserved manner with which he received her more facetious questions, that the brakes were in order, or had been when the car was brought out of the garage.

"Well, then, pull up," said his employer. "Something has happened on the seaward side of the road. I think someone's gone over the edge."

Her keen sight, and a certain sensitivity she had to visual impressions, had not deceived her. She followed the track of a bicycle to the edge of the cliff, crouched, lay flat, and looked over.

Below her the seagulls screamed, and, farther down, the sea flung sullenly, despite the brilliant day, against the heavy rocks, or whirlpooled, snarling, about the black island promontories, for the tide was on the turn and coming in fast. Sea-pinks, some of them brown and withered now, for their season was almost past, clung in the crevices or grew in the smallest hollows of the cliff-face. Near one root of them a paper bag had lodged. Had it been empty, the west wind, blowing freshly along the face of the cliff (which looked north to the Bristol Channel), must have removed it almost as soon as it alighted, but there it perched, not wedged, yet heavy enough to hold its place against the breeze. To the left of it, about four yards off, was a deep, dark stain, visible because it was on the only piece of white stone that could be seen.

"Odd," said Mrs. Bradley, and began to perform the feat which she would not have permitted to anyone under her control — that of climbing down to reach the dark-stained rock.

The stain was certainly blood, and was still slightly sticky to the touch. She looked farther down (having, fortunately, a mountaineer's head for heights) and thought that, some thirty feet below her, she could see a piece of cloth. It was caught on the only bush which seemed to have found root and sustenance upon the rocky cliff. It resembled, she thought, material of which a man's suit might be made.

She left it where it was and scrambled across to the bag.

×

"George," she said, when she had regained the dark, overhanging lip of the rough turf edge of the cliff and had discovered her chauffeur at the top, "I think I saw a public telephone marked on the map. Somebody ought to search the shore below these cliffs, I rather fancy."

"It would need to be by boat, then, madam. The tide comes up the foot," replied the chauffeur. He began to walk back up the hill.

Mrs. Bradley sat down at the roadside and waited for him to return. While she was waiting she untwisted the top of the screwed-up paper bag and examined the contents with interest.

She found a packet of safety-razor blades, a tube of toothpaste half-full, a face flannel, a wrapped cake of soap of the dimensions known euphemistically in the advertisements as "guest-size," a very badly worn toothbrush, a set of small buttons on a card, a pipe-cleaner, half a bicycle bell, two rubber patches for mending punctures, and a piece of wormlike valve-rubber.

"Calculated to indicate that whoever left the bag there was a cyclist, George," she observed, when her chauffeur came back from the telephone. "Of course, nobody may have fallen over the cliff, but what do you make of the marks?"

"Palmer tyres, gent's model not enough clearance for a lady's see where the pedal caught the edge of the turf?"

"Yes, George. Unfortunately one loses the track a yard from the side of the road. I should have supposed that the bicycle would have left a better account of itself if it had really been ridden over. Besides, what could have made anybody ride it over the edge? The road is wide enough, and there does not seem to be much traffic. I think perhaps I'll retrieve that piece of cloth before we go."

"I most seriously hope you will not, madam, if you'll excuse me. I've no head for heights myself or I would get it. After all, we know just where it is. The police could get it later, with ropes and tackle for their men, if it should be required at an inquest."

"Very true, George. Let us get on to the village to see whether a boat has put out. How much farther is it?"

"Another three miles and a half, madam. There's another hill after this a smaller one."

The car descended decorously. The hill dropped sheer and steep for about another half-mile, and then it twisted suddenly away to the right, so that an inn which was on the left-hand side at the bend appeared, for an instant, to be standing in the middle of the road.

So far as the black-haired girl on the smashed and buckled tandem was concerned, that was where it might as well have stood, Mrs. Bradley reflected. The tandem had been ridden straight into a brick wall slap into it as though the rider had been blind or as though the machine she was riding had been completely out of her control. Whatever the cause of the accident, she had hurtled irrevocably to her death, or so Mrs. Bradley thought when first she knelt beside her.

"Rat-trap pedals, of all things, madam," said George. The plump large feet in the centre-seamed cycling shoes were still caught in the bent steel traps. George tested the brakes.

"The brakes don't act," he said. "Perhaps a result of the accident, madam, although I shouldn't think so." He released the girl's feet and lifted the tandem away. Mrs. Bradley, first delicately and then with slightly more firmness, sought for injuries.

"George," she said, "the case of instruments. And then go and get some cold water from somewhere or other."

The girl had a fractured skull. Her left leg was slightly lacerated, but it was not bruised and the bone was not broken. Her face was unmarked, except by the dirt from the roadside. It was all a little out of the ordinary, Mrs. Bradley thought, seizing the thermos flask full of icy water which the resourceful George had brought from a moorland stream.

"She's alive, George, I think," she said. "But there have been some very odd goings-on. Are the tandem handlebars locked?"

"No, madam. They move freely."

"Don't you think the front wheel should have been more seriously affected?"

"Why, yes, perhaps it should, madam. The young woman can't go much less than ten or eleven stone, and with the brakes out of order."

"And although her feet were caught in the rat-trap pedals, her face isn't even marked. It was only a little dirty before I washed it."

"Sounds like funny business, madam, to me."

"And to me, too, George. Is there a hospital near? We must have an ambulance if possible. I don't think the car will do. She ought to lie flat. That skull wants trepanning and at once. Mind how you go down the hill, though. I'll stay here with her. You might leave me a fairly heavy spanner."

Left alone with the girl, Mrs. Bradley fidgeted with her case of instruments, took out gouge forceps, sighed, shook her head, and put them back again. The wound on the top of the head was extremely puzzling. A fracture of the base of the skull would have been the most likely head injury, unless the girl had crashed head-first into the wall, but, from the position in which the body had been lying, this seemed extremely unlikely. One other curious point Mrs. Bradley noticed which changed her suppositions into certainty. The elastic-waisted white blouse and the shorts met neatly. It was impossible to believe that they could do so unless they had been pulled together after the girl had fallen from the saddle.

Mrs. Bradley made a mental picture of the girl leaning forward over the low-slung sports-type handlebars of the machine. She must, in the feminine phrase, have "come apart' at the back. That blouse could never have overlapped those shorts.

Interested and curious, Mrs. Bradley turned up the edge of the soiled white blouse. There was nothing underneath it but the bare brown skin marked with two or three darker moles at the waist. Of the bright pink vest there was no sign; neither had the girl a knapsack or any kind of luggage into which she could have stuffed the vest supposing that she had taken it off for coolness.

"Odd," said Mrs. Bradley gain, weighing the spanner thoughtfully in her hand. "I wonder what's happened to the husband?"

At this moment there came round the bend an A.A. scout wheeling a bicycle. He saluted as he came nearer.

"Oh dear, madam! Nasty accident here! Poor young woman! Anything I can do?"

"Yes," said Mrs. Bradley very promptly. "Get an ambulance. I'm afraid she's dead, but there might be a chance if you're quick. No, don't touch her. I'm a doctor. I've done all that can be done here. Hurry, please. Every moment is important."

"No ambulance in the village, madam. Couldn't expect it, could you? I might perhaps be able to get a car. How did you get here? Was you with her when she crashed?"

"Go and get a car. A police car, if you like. Dead or alive, she'll have to be moved as soon as possible."

"Yes, she will, won't she?" said the man. He turned his bicycle, and, mounting it, shot away round the bend.

Mrs. Bradley unfolded an Ordnance Survey map of the district and studied it closely. Then she took out a reading glass and studied it again. She put out a yellow claw and traced the line of the road she was on, and followed it into the village towards which first George and then the A.A. scout had gone.

The road ran on uncompromisingly over the thin red contour lines of the map, past nameless bays on one side and the shoulder of the moor on a rising hill on the other. Of deviations from it there were none; not so much as the dotted line of a moorland track, not even a stream, gave any indication that there might be other ways of reaching the village besides crossing the open moorland or keeping to the line of the road. There was nothing marked on the map but the cliffs and the shore on the one hand, the open hill country on the other.

She was still absorbed when George returned with the car.

"The village has no ambulance, madam, but the bus has decanted its passengers on to the bridge and is getting here as fast as it can. It was thought in the village, madam, that the body could be laid along one of the seats."

"I hope and trust that body is but a relative term. The young woman will live, George, I fancy. Somebody has had his trouble for nothing."

"I am glad to hear that, madam. The villagers seem well-disposed, and the bus is the best they can do."

He spoke of the villagers as though they were the aboriginal inhabitants of some country which was still in the process of being explored. Mrs. Bradley gave a harsh little snort of amusement and then observed,

"Did the A.A. scout stop and speak to you? Or did you ask him for information?"

"No, madam, neither at all. He was mending a puncture when I passed him."

"Was that on your journey to the village or on the return here?"

"Just now, madam. I saw no one on my journey to the village."

"Interesting," said Mrs. Bradley, thinking of her Ordnance map. "Punctures are a nuisance, George, are they not? If you see him again you might ask him whether Daisy Bell met her husband on top of the hill."

Just then the bus arrived. Off it jumped a police sergeant and a constable, who, under Mrs. Bradley's direction, lifted the girl and placed her on one of the seats, of which the bus had two, running the whole of the inside length of the vehicle.

"You take the car to the hotel, George. I'll be there as soon as I can," said his employer. "Now, constable, we have to hold her as still as we can. Sergeant, kindly instruct the driver to avoid the bumps in the road, and then come in here and hold my coat to screen the light from her head. Is there a hospital in the village?"

"No, ma'am. There's a home for inebriates, though. That's the nearest thing. We're going to take her there, and Constable Fogg is fetching Doctor MacBain."

"Splendid," said Mrs. Bradley, and devoted herself thenceforward entirely to her patient.

One morning some days later, when the mist had cleared from the moors and the sun was shining on every drop of moisture, she sent for the car, and thus addressed her chauffeur:

"Well, did you give the scout my message?"

"Yes, madam, but he did not comprehend it."

"Indeed? And did you explain?"

"No, madam, not being instructed."

"Excellent, child. We shall drive to the fatal spot, and there we shall see what we shall see."

George, looking haughty because he felt befogged, held open the door of the car, and Mrs. Bradley put her foot on the step.

"I'll sit in front, George," she said.

The car began to mount slowly to the bend where the accident had come to their notice. George was pulling up, but his employer invited him to go on.

"Our goal is the top of the hill, George. That is where they were to meet, you remember. That is the proper place from which to begin our inquiry. Is it not strange and interesting to consider all the motives for murder and attempted murder that come to men's minds? To women's minds, too, of course. The greater includes the less."

She cackled harshly. George who (although he would have found it difficult to account for his opinion) had always conceived her to be an ardent feminist, looked at the road ahead, and did not relax his expression of dignified aloofness.

Prevented, by the fact that he was driving, from poking him in the ribs (her natural reaction to an attitude such as the one he was displaying), Mrs. Bradley grinned tigerishly, and the car crawled on up the worst and steepest part of the gradient.

George then broke his silence.

"In my opinion, madam, no young woman losing her brakes on such a hill could have got off so light as she did, nor that tandem either."

"True, George."

"If you will excuse the question, madam, what put the idea of an attempt on her into your mind?"

"I suppose the piscina, George."

George concluded that she was amusing herself at his expense and accepted the reply for what it was worth, which to him was nothing, since he did not know what a piscina was (and was habitually averse to seeking such information). He drove on a little faster as the gradient eased to one in seven and then to one in ten.

"Just here, George," said his employer. "Run off on to the turf on the right-hand side."

George pulled up very close to the A.A. telephone which he had used before. Here the main road cut away from the route they had traversed and an A.A. scout was on duty at the junction.

"Behind the barn, down on my knees," observed Mrs. Bradley, chanting the words in what she fondly believed to be accents of their origin, "I thought I heard a chicken sneeze, and I did, too. Come and look at this, George."

It was the bright pink vest. There was no mistaking it, although it was stained now, messily and rustily, with blood.

"Not her blood, George; his," remarked Mrs. Bradley. "I wonder he dared bring it back here, all the same. And I wonder where the young woman the first time fell off the tandem?" She looked again at the blood-stained vest. "He must have cut himself badly, but, of course, he had to get enough blood to make the white stone look impressive, and he wanted the vest to smear it on with so that he need use nothing of his own. Confused thinking, George, on the whole, but murderers do think confusedly, and one can feel for them, of course."

She sent George to fetch the A.A. scout, who observed,

"Was it the young woman as fell off bottom of Countsferry? Must have had a worse tumble just here by the box than Stanley seemed to think. He booked the tumble in his private log. Would you be the young woman's relatives, ma'am?"

"We represent her interests," said Mrs. Bradley, remarking afterwards to George that she thought they might consider themselves as doing so since they had saved her life.

"Well, he's left the log with me, and it do seem to show the cause of her shaking up. Must have been dazed like, and not seen the bend as it was coming, and run herself into the wall. And Stanley, they do say, must have gone over the cliff in trying to save her, for he ain't been back on duty any more. Cruel, these parts, they be."

"Did her fall upset her brakes, then?" Mrs. Bradley inquired. She read the laconic entry in the exercise book presented for her inspection and, having earned the scout's gratitude in the customary simple manner, she returned to the car with the vest (which the scout had not seen) pushed into the large pocket of her skirt.

"Stop at the scene of the accident, George," she said. "She seemed," said George admiringly later on to those who were standing him a pint in exchange for the story, "like a bloodhound on the murderer's trail."

"For a murderer he was, in intention, if not in fact," continued George, taking, without his own knowledge, a recognised though debatable ecclesiastical view. "She climbed up the bank and on to the moor as if she knew just what to look for, madam did. She showed me the very stone she reckoned he hit the young woman over the head with, and then where he sunk in the soft earth deeper than his first treads, because he was carrying the body back to the tandem to make out she crashed and fell off."

"And didn't she crash?" his hearers wanted to know.

"Crash? What her? A young woman who, to give her her due (although I don't hold with such things), had cycled that tandem sport model and meant for two men all the way down there from London? No. He crashed the tandem himself after he'd done her in. That was to deceive the police or anybody else that found her. He followed her on his bike down the hill with the deed in his heart. You see, he was her husband.

"But he didn't deceive me and madam, not by a long chalk he didn't! Why, first thing I said to her, I said, 'Didn't it ought to be buckled up more than that if she came down that hill without brakes?' 'Course, that was his little mistake. That, and using her vest. I hope they give him ten years!

"Well, back we went up the hill to where madam found the paper bag and its etceteras. The only blood we could see was on the only white stone."

The barmaid at this point begged him to stop. He gave her the horrors, she said.

"So what?" one listener inquired.

"Well, the whole bag of tricks was to show that someone, and that someone a man and a cyclist, had gone over the cliff and was killed, like the other scout said. That was going to be our scout's alibi if the police ever got on his track, so madam thinks, but he hoped he wouldn't need to use that; it was just his stand-by, like. The other A.A. man had seen him go off duty. That was his danger, or so he thought, not reckoning on madam and me. He'd fixed the head of the young woman's machine while she stood talking to him at the A.A. telephone, so that when she mounted it threw her. That was to show (that's why he logged it, see?) as she mightn't have been herself when she took the bend. Pretty little idea."

Three days later Mrs. Bradley said to him, "They will be able to establish motive at the trial, George. Bell I call him that was arrested yesterday evening. He had insured his wife, it appears, as soon as they were married, and wished to obtain possession of the money."

"But what I would still like to know, madam," George observed, "is what put the thought of murder into your mind before ever we saw the accident or even the bag and the blood."

"The bag and the blood, for some reason, sounds perfectly horrible, George."

"But, madam, you spotted the marks he'd made on that edge with his push-bike as though you'd been waiting to spot them. And you fixed on him as the murderer, too, straight away."

"Ah, that was easy, George. You see, he'd never mentioned that he'd seen you go by in his car, and you told me that on your journey to the village to find assistance you had not seen him either. Therefore, since he must have been somewhere along that road, I asked myself why, even if he should have left the roadside himself, his bicycle should not have been visible. Besides, he was the perfect answer to several questions which, up to that time, I had had to ask myself. One was: why did they choose to meet at the top of that hill? Another was: why did he risk bending over the injured girl to fix her feet back in those rat-trap pedals we saw and out of which, I should imagine, her feet would most certainly have been pulled if she'd had such a very bad crash?"

"Ah, yes, the A.A. box and the A.A. uniform, madam. In other words, Mr. G.K. Chesterton's postman all over again."

"Precisely, George. The obvious meeting place, in the circumstances, and the conspicuous yet easily forgotten uniform."

"But, madam, if I may revert, what did turn your mind to murder?"

"The piscina, George," Mrs. Bradley solemnly reminded him. George looked at her, hesitated, then overrode the habit of years and inquired,

"What is a piscina, madam?"

"A drain, George. Merely a drain.

"Now, body, turn to air,
Or Lucifer will bear thee quick to hell!
O soul, be chang'd into little water drops,
And fall into the ocean, ne'er be found!"

Strangers' Hall

No, it did not happen in Norfolk, but you will know (if you know Norwich) why I choose to give my tale that title. My home was in a small place called Itchen Market, in Hampshire, and I got my house very cheap on condition that I was willing to show it to American visitors — to English or any other visitors, too, for the matter of that — and would keep it well looked after.

The house was built in the early sixteenth-century, but on an older foundation. The cellars and part of the ground floor are thirteenth-century and incredibly gloomy, with grained stone ceilings and oddly-shaped nooks and corners. Visitors were always very much impressed by the fact that I had laid out these parts of the house to look as I imagined they would have looked when the first owners lived here.

That is to say, I had great strewings of rushes on the stone floors, a piece of quite respectable tapestry (sixteenth-century Flemish, but good enough for a spot of local colour) on two of the walls, and on the central hearth a reasonably realistic arrangement of logs on a kind of double trivet. I made this trivet myself on my little forge, and I was rather proud of it.

I didn't get many visitors, and when they came I always showed them round myself. With the assistance of the vicar, I prepared a small handbook and I printed it last year on my little press. I always gave people a copy when they were leaving, as I could scarcely demand a gratuity, and people often took the hint and put down some money rather furtively on the table on which I kept a little pile of the books. After all, I was retired on a not very large pension, every little helped, and there was nothing in my agreement against it.

A short while ago a big liner docked at Southampton and I hoped for custom. My house was at least twenty miles from the docks, but I had long had my illustrated advertisements at Southampton and Bournemouth, so there was really no excuse for anyone not knowing of the existence of my gem of a house.

Luck was in. The weather turned wet, and by the end of the afternoon I had had no fewer than five parties and was feeling tired but pleased. I had netted three pounds sixteen and six-pence — a splendid haul — and had had a thoroughly entertaining afternoon. A gentleman from Kentucky, who was accompanied by his wife and a son of fourteen, asked permission to take photographs and left a couple of guineas; another party left ten shillings, after a rather broad hint from me; the third lot gave three and six — a father and his college-age son, who argued (not too quietly) about whether they should contribute or not; and the fourth party left a pound. The fifth and last party cashed in for a shilling. They were a Cockney fellow and his girl. Neither of them thought much of the house, and it was quite good of them to give me anything at all. I was told to buy myself a beer. It was very kindly meant, and they obviously thought they were doing a handsome thing. I was rather delighted with them, and invited them to stay for tea.

By tea-time the rain was a deluge and they were glad to stay in the dry. Hardly had they left — they had a coach to catch at six o'clock — when a sixth party arrived, but not with the idea of viewing the house. It was a motorist who had stopped to ask the way to the London road. Our village is not on one of the great highways and after heavy rain motorists did some times knock on my door, because our water-splash is apt to deepen dangerously. I lived nearest to it — my house is remote from the village — and naturally people inquired of me for another way round. This was not easy to describe, so I always offered to get into the car and accompany them, directing the car as we went. It made a little change for me to ride in a car, and I didn't in the least mind walking back by the short cut over the water-splash. It has a narrow footbridge, of no use to cars but a very present help to pedestrians.

I found that these little acts of kindness did much to alleviate the monotony of my days. After all, I used to drive a car myself once. They also evoked gratitude, but I was somewhat surprised when my new acquaintance, a middle-aged man with an aura of worldliness and wealth, stopped the car and would not immediately consent to my departure.

One reads of dreadful things happening to people who accept lifts in cars and I usually went prepared, but this man gave me his case of cigars (and I do dearly love my Corona y Corona when I can get it without paying for it), gave me his City address and the name of a man in Southampton who would let me have Scotch, and we parted at just after seven. It did not take me long to reach home, but I was soaked to the skin and had to put my feet into hot mustard and water to avoid taking cold.

The motorist's mention of whisky also tempted me to take out a black bottle (which I kept for emergencies) and treat myself to a couple of powerful preventives, and it was with a feeling of great well-being that I settled with my book in front of the small fireplace which I kept hidden away behind a huge Tudor façade in my bedroom, and threw on a couple more logs.

Time passed, and the next thing I knew was the clock striking eleven. Now I am an early bird as a rule. There is not a great deal of pleasure to be obtained from the light of candles or a paraffin lamp. The consequence was that with me early to bed was early to rise, and in summer I was usually up by five.

Although, contrary to custom, I had gone late to bed, the next morning was no exception to my rule. I awoke to find my uncurtained room dimly lit by the dawn, and after an enjoyable, short, lazy spell, I arose, washed the sleep from my eyes under the pump in the yard, and then began my morning labours.

Ordinarily I completely changed the rushes in the cellar and ground-floor rooms once a fortnight, but after a wet day I always swept them up into great heaps, loaded them into sacks, took them up into my big shed, which has a brick floor, and sorted them over.

I threw away any very dirty ones, replaced the rest, and added straw if necessary to make up the amount. This was a before-breakfast job and took me every bit of an hour and a half.

On this particular occasion it took me less than twenty minutes. I always crossed to the far end of the cellar and swept towards the door. Now, in one of the embrasures in the cellar I kept an oak bench. It had nothing to do with the period in which the cellar was built. As a matter of fact, it was made in the nineteenth century by a village craftsman in Sussex, but it was an honest job of work and looked quite in keeping.

It seemed to me that a whole heap of rushes had got kicked up in front of this bench, and as soon as I'd cleared the far end of the cellar I went at the bench with great energy, and immediately discovered the reason for the heap of rushes.

The heap of rushes hid a body. Not a live body; a dead body. And not only a dead body but an obviously murdered body. It was horrible. It was so horrible that I dropped the hard broom, got to the little staircase, climbed up into the fresh air of my kitchen garden, and was terribly sick.

I felt better after that. The first horror passed. I began to wonder what I should do. The police and a doctor — that was my first thought. But I live alone and the police do jump to such peculiar and strange conclusions. They might have thought me guilty.

I sat down, feeling very weak and not too clear-headed, but suddenly the great decision was formed. Living in the next village was a very famous woman psychiatrist. She was a doctor, too, and sometimes assisted the police in tracking down murderers who might otherwise have gone undetected. She had once brought one of her relatives over to see my house. I could claim to say that I knew her.

I went to the telephone — the one modern installation in my ancient dwelling — and, after looking her up in the book, I rang Mrs. Bradley's house at Wandles Parva. She was at home. She was up. She would come. Much restored, I ventured into the cellar again and took another look at the horror which still lay, dreadfully dead, among my heaped and dirty rushes.

The head injuries were shocking. The face, I felt very sure, was no longer recognisable. I touched nothing, of course, but I forced myself to notice everything so that I could tell the police (who, of course, would have to come sooner or later) every possible detail.

Mrs. Bradley came just forty minutes after I had telephoned. Her chauffeur, a sturdy, reliable-looking fellow, had driven her over, and, like a faithful watchdog, he followed her into the house.

We went straight down to the cellar. It is lighted by two high holes at ground level and two large lanterns which hang from iron wall-brackets, but Mrs. Bradley had brought a powerful torch. The chauffeur held it whilst she knelt and examined the body. It was a repulsive job for an elderly woman, but she gave no sign of finding it anything out of the ordinary.

"How long do you suppose he's been dead?" she asked, fixing me with her keen, black eyes. I said I had no idea. Laymen are not commonly expert in these matters. She cackled — an unexpected sound in that little charnel-house — and added, in practical tones: "Well, did you have an accomplice to get him down here?"

Reassured by her tone, I ventured to ask whether the man had not been killed in the cellar.

"I do not think so," she replied briskly. "There would have been plenty of blood, of which I see no sign, and your rushes are dirty. It is obvious that you have not changed them for some days. I've seen everything here that matters. Let us go upstairs, shall we, and, before the police arrive — I called them, of course, as soon as I had your message — you shall tell me everything you can."

In a few moments we were seated in my dining-room. Mrs. Bradley had breakfasted. I was still feeling quite disinclined for food. I settled myself eagerly to answer all she wished to ask me.

"I am assuming that the body was not there yesterday when your many visitors brought in all that mud on their shoes," she began.

I was surprised she should have realised that I had had a large number of visitors, but the trained eye, no doubt, takes in a vast amount of detail at a glance, and there was certainly plenty of mud and water on the floor.

"I don't see how he could have been there yesterday," I said. "You are right in saying that I had a number of visitors. One in particular, a fourteen-year-old American lad, scuffled his feet freely among the rushes and investigated everything with transatlantic thoroughness. I hardly think a corpse would have gone unnoticed by him."

"It seems unlikely. Besides, the man's clothes are still soaking. Now we can conclude that none of these visitors brought the body with him and left it behind when he went. It was placed in your cellar at some time between when your last visitor left, and the early hours of this morning. When were you out of the house?"

This question was distinctly uncanny. She must have read my mind, for, as she spoke, I was thinking of the smooth stranger whose car I had directed on to the London road.

"That's when it happened! He kept me talking while confederates dumped the body in my cellar!" I exclaimed. "I didn't think of locking my front door. I never do until it's dark. Anybody would only need to lift up the latch and walk in. It must have been somebody who knew the house. Good heavens! It must have been one of my afternoon visitors! What do you think about that?"

"Do you keep a visitors' book?" she enquired.

I went immediately to get it. She perused the entries for the previous day with apparent interest.

"I should think we could leave the Americans out of it," I ventured. She nodded, took out a small magnifying glass and scrutinised the signatures closely.

"The difficulty will be to get him identified," she said. "Describe to me A. F. and K. G. Stepson."

I gave her what account I could of the rather parsimonious father and son.

"And this man whom you directed on to the London road — are you certain that you've never seen him before?"

"I don't remember having done so."

"Would you recognise him if you saw him again?"

"Oh, yes, I certainly should. He was very cordial, and we talked for some little time, as I explained to you. I am sure now that he was detaining me deliberately. Why, we even had a long argument as to his giving me his case of cigars."

"I wonder what happened to him after you parted?"

"Well," I said, summoning a smile, "we can hardly answer that question. We know only what his confederates did"

"I wish we had a clue to his identity. You said he gave you his cigar-case? I wonder whether I might see it?"

It was lying on my sideboard, where I had laid it the night before. It was quite a good case, and bore what I had taken to be a regimental badge.

"This might help a bit," I suggested. She fixed me with an eye like a gimlet.

"It certainly will," she replied. "Would it surprise you to know that this same crest is painted on the door of a car which is at present standing marooned in the middle of your water-splash? My man and I examined it before we entered your house."

"But cars — private cars — don't have regimental crests!" I objected.

"Exactly. I think we may take it for granted that your unwanted guest downstairs is the owner of the marooned car, don't you? — And that he could have been pitched down into your cellar quite easily through one of the ground-level lights?"

"Well — well, yes, if you say so," I stammered. I was absolutely dumbfounded. "But how on earth did the car get into the water-splash, I wonder?"

"It was driven back from the London road and into the water-splash deliberately. The water is three feet deep and has washed out most of the bloodstains. It is unfortunate for the murderer that it also stopped the engine." She turned to the chauffeur. "George!"

The stolid man searched me rapidly whilst she, the black-eyed termagant, held me with fingers of steel. They found the wallet, of course.

"I suppose you saw this when he pulled out a visiting card to scribble down the address of the purveyor of Scotch," she remarked. "Like most people who live alone, you're far too garrulous, you know. All right, George. We may relax. I hear the police at the door."

Beast and devil! Beast! Filthy, feline devil! The police took me out to the car. Their questions completely broke me down. After all, I had never been in their hands before. Then they hauled out the car and showed me. I had agreed to the man's identity for nothing. That she-fiend had outwitted me. There was no crest on the car at all.

They also found my defensive weapon — I'll swear that's all I ever intended it to be — my little iron blackjack I had made on my own little forge. It was among the waterlogged tools of the car, but it seems that water does not wash fingerprints away.

A Light on Murder

The body had been there for five days, and the men in the lighthouse could not get to it. Their relief was overdue, but before any of them looked southward for the welcome sight of their boat, he would first look to the west, to the black rocks against whose smooth-washed crevices the pale face and hands of the dead man showed up like pieces of paper.

They had no doubt of the identity of the corpse. They who had been four were now three. At night the great light, revolving its god-like eye, would pick out the form of their comrade, and then, as though to hide the sight from everything save the stars, it would sweep on until the next revolution again revealed the unthinkable thought — that Dick was dead.

"He must have jumped," said Tom, the oldest and most experienced of the men. "It's a bad thing for Maggie. Who's to tell her?"

"Funny how the sea picked him up and chucked him on the rocks and then never swept him off again," said Dugald, the youngest man.

"It seems as if he'd been there a year," said Walt, who was almost new to the lighthouse. "I wonder what his trouble was? He never said anything, did he?"

"You don't need to have trouble to do a thing like that," said old Tom. "It takes fellows that way sometimes. You get browned-off on a light. Then you get to looking down at the sea from the gallery round the lamp, and then you do it. I knew a fellow once on the Dymballs — But Dick never seemed that sort."

The relief boat arrived two days later, and, in spite of a still-heavy swell, it took the dead man from the rocks. But when the captain looked at the body he refused to take anybody off the lighthouse. He returned to shore with poor Dick as fast as his boat could churn the seas. There was a knife between the dead man's shoulder-blades.

The police went out to the lighthouse and questioned the three keepers. It was soon proved that the knife had been the property of the dead man himself, but as it was impossible that be could have thrust it into his own back, there remained the question: which of his three companions had murdered him?

The fingerprints of all three men were taken but proved useless. There were no prints on the haft of the knife, and in the lamp-room and on the gallery (the only two places in which the murder was at all likely to have been committed unless more than one of the men had been concerned in it) there were the prints of all the keepers, the dead man himself included, on the railings and on the gear.

Kitbags, lockers and clothes were minutely inspected for traces of blood, but the wound had not bled very much, and when no such traces were found nobody was particularly surprised.

Medical evidence at the inquest established that the man had been dead for eight or nine days. This coincided with the story of the keepers that about thirty-six hours after Dick had disappeared his body had been seen on the rocks and was there seven days. There was no other evidence worth considering, so the police decided to take the line that all three men were equally guilty of murder. No arrest was made, but the men were closely tailed and were not sent back to their duty.

"But, of course, they're not all guilty," said the Inspector in charge of the case, "and what we have got to do is to sort out the wheat from the chaff. The sooner the better, too. Trinity House don't like it that we've practically pinched three of their men. But we can't have them back on the light to destroy or to fake the evidence. But how to get at the truth — "

"We want a psychologist, sir," said his bright young sergeant from Hendon. "Why don't we brief Mrs. Lestrange Bradley?"

"Mrs. How-Much?"

"Lestrange Bradley, sir. The psychologist. Her specialty is solving murder cases."

"Oh — her. Yes, well, it might be an idea. I don't like the thought of jugging an honest chap like a blinking prize turkey at a show."

Mrs. Bradley was interested in her new task. The men, at her instigation, were taken, one at a time, to revisit the light house in her company. The fact that two police officers in plain clothes accompanied each man was neither here nor there. Nothing was said on either side.

Mrs. Bradley took the men in reverse order of age. She was anxious to present old Tom (whom, privately and off the record, she did not suspect of the murder) with the evidence of the other two as a guarantee of and a check upon their truthfulness. His long experience of light-house work would be invaluable, she decided.

Young Dugald was her first victim. He was a red-haired, raw-looking, chunky man of twenty-eight, married, with two children. The dead man had been thirty-two, not very happily married, and without children. As the keepers were relieved on a rota, there might possibly have been trouble, Mrs. Bradley thought, if Dick had known Dugald's wife.

"We wass neffer relieved at the same time, Dick and myself," said Dugald, gazing out to sea with his warm, green-hazel eyes, and speaking in the sing-song voice of West Scotland. "But we wass friendly, for all tha-at. I would not serve Dick a dirty turn, Cruachan, no! Not for gold!"

"Well, if you didn't, who did?" Mrs. Bradley inquired briskly, for she dreaded a Highland lament for the dead man. Dugald turned his head and looked thoughtfully at her. He saw a black-eyed, yellow-skinned, elderly woman, not at all prepossessing to look at. Her appearance did not seem to affect him. He had not a very high standard of physical beauty.

"I will wish to be knowing that, myself," he replied. "You see, it was this way." He paused, collecting his thoughts. "The pollissmen haff put it all out of my head," he said sadly. "It wass so clear before all the argument."

Mrs. Bradley could believe this. She waited patiently.

"You see, it wass this way," Dugald repeated in his soft, sad tones. "Dick wass on duty in the lamp-room, and the three of us, we wass in the bunk-room. Dick wass on duty from da-ark until midnight, then I wass to be on until two, Walt from two until four, and Tom from four until daylight." Mrs. Bradley made a note of these times.

"But when I went up to relieve him, the poor man was gone," concluded Dugald. "He wass not there. There wass no one." So Dick had been killed before midnight. That was fact, unless contradicted later, Mrs. Bradley noted.

"Yes, I see," she said encouragingly. "Did anything else happen that was out of the ordinary?"

"Well, you see, it wass a queer thing, so it wass, and I do not remember it happening effer before, but while Dick wass on duty that efening all of us, myself too, wass not feeling ferra well, and we went out from the bunk-room — but it is not manners I should be telling this to a lady."

"But I understand perfectly," Mrs. Bradley assured him. "You all had upset stomachs, and a need to leave the bunk-room. No explanation is necessary. You are telling me that, in your opinion, any one of you could have killed Dick. Were you all absent long enough for that?"

"You wouldn't watch the clock on such an occasion," explained Dugald. "You would be trying to sleep until you would need to go outside to be sick."

Mrs. Bradley nodded.

"And you were on duty immediately after Dick," she remarked in an innocent tone. Dugald gave her a quick glance.

"That is so," he replied. "But, my sorrow! You must not be thinking I killed the poor man! Ochen, och, no! I would neffer haff been doing that! By Cruachan, no!"

Mrs. Bradley accepted this denial with tolerant indifference, and Dugald was taken off. She spent the intervening time in drinking tea with the relief men — three instead of the usual four — and in being taken on an exhaustive tour of the lighthouse. She was shown the great lamp and received an explanation of its workings. She inspected the fog-signals apparatus, and did an immense amount of climbing up and down the spiral iron staircase and in gazing at the sea through unexpected windows which lit the upper floors of the tower.

She was particularly interested in the domestic side of the keepers' lonely lives. She saw the galley and received details of food, cooking, washing up, and laundering.

"You must all be a great comfort to your wives and mothers," she remarked as she sat down on one of the bunks. The men grinned.

"Funny thing," one of them remarked, "but it's the single ones that are handiest at cooking the grub. It's the married chaps as does the chores."

"I suppose it is understandable that the single men should be cooks," Mrs. Bradley observed. "They are the ones who often have to fend for themselves on shore."

One of the men agreed and the other one debated the point. The third man was on duty, for a watch had to be kept, and the log written up, by day as well as by night.

Soon the boat which had taken off Dugald returned with Walt. Mrs. Bradley took him and his police escort up to the lamp-room again, as that seemed to her, as well as to the police, the most likely place for the murder. There was no doubt that the dead man had been on duty when he was killed; that is, if Dugald's evidence could be trusted; and it could easily be refuted by the others if he were lying. In any case, the gallery outside the lamp-room was easily the simplest place from which the body could have been tumbled into the sea. She looked forward to her interview with Walt.

Walt was a tough-looking six-foot man with fair hair and grey-blue eyes. He measured up the little old woman with a quick, sardonic stare, and shrugged his broad shoulders as he answered her first question offhandedly.

"Why, Duggie told us," he said. "He had to go on duty at twelve, but I reckon he took his time getting up there, because we all — well, p'raps he told you."

"Yes, I've had that point put to me," Mrs. Bradley replied. "You are about to tell me, I think, that although Dugald went to take over his watch before you were compelled to leave the bunk-room for the second or third time, you had returned to the bunk-room before he came down with the news that Dick was not to be found, and you thought him a long time gone."

"No, it was the first time with me, but I reckon he wasn't gone as long as I thought. Besides, I don't blame him. It's no odds to anybody if a chap goes into the galley to see whether there's another cup of cocoa left in the jug, and hots it up before he goes on duty, and takes it up there with him."

"So the mug was up there in the lamp-room when you and Tom went up?"

"I can't remember whether it was or not. What odds, anyway?"

"None, probably. How did the two men get on?"

"What, Duggie and Dick? All right, so far as I know. You *have* to get on with the other blokes on a light."

"I should imagine so. Yet someone didn't hit it off with Dick."

"I can't make it out," said Walt.

The relief crew looked at the small elderly woman and the tall young man with some curiosity as they came back into the bunk-room with their escort. The plain-clothes officers then went off with Walt, took him ashore to the waiting police car and brought off old Tom to the light.

"Are you any forwarder, mam?" old Tom enquired when he had been disembarked at the lighthouse steps and had climbed to the galley for a mug of tea before Mrs. Bradley questioned him.

"I shall be, by the time you go back," she answered. "No, none for me, Tom, thank you. I've already had some with the relief men."

"I'll be glad to be back on here," said old Tom wistfully. "Rough on my missus, this is. She bears up well, but it's the disgrace. It'll get her down if things don't go right and I'm arrested. And one of us'll have to be, won't we?"

"It would interest me very much to know your opinion as to which one, Tom," said Mrs. Bradley. "Who did it? Who committed the murder? You must have a pretty shrewd idea."

But Tom was staunch. All three men had already been asked by the police (indirectly, of course, but sufficiently plainly) this very same question. None would give another away.

"Thinking ain't knowing," said Tom. "All I know is the one that *didn't* do it, and that there one is me. But all that's got to be proved."

"Do you all carry knives around with you? Does a man have his knife with him all the time?"

"Yes, I reckon we always have a knife on us. It comes in handy, and a man don't always want to be climbing up and down them stairs, especially at my age."

"I suppose not. What do you do with yourselves when you're off duty?"

"I dunno as we ever are off duty much in the daytime. On *and* off, as you might say. We don't reckon much on an eight-hour day, or anything of that kind, off here. We cooks and mends and washes and swabs up and plays cards and does knitting. I be the champion knitter and mender, and Dick, he were chief handyman. Dugald and him done the swabbing up, too, and Walt were main handy in the galley."

"So Dugald and Dick were more often together on the job than either of you others?"

"Well," said Tom, choosing his words, "that might be so, but it weren't nothing to signify, and they always seemed to rub along all right."

"Yes, I see. Now, Tom, there's one more thing. Dugald had to take over the duty from Dick at midnight."

"Ay, that's right."

"He went up to the lamp-room, found that Dick had disappeared — or so he says — "

"I reckon he meant it," said Tom, in a tone of obstinacy. Mrs. Bradley, having made the point, abandoned it.

"How long was he gone before he came down and told you two that Dick had disappeared?"

Tom searched her quick black eyes, but they told him nothing.

"I couldn't rightly say," he replied. "But I reckon he didn't go straight up. We'd often hot up a drink for ourselves and take the jug and two mugs up with us — one for the bloke on watch and the other for ourself, and drink it together before the watch came down to turn in."

"Did you see a jug and two mugs up there in the lamp-room, Tom, when Dugald called you that night to say Dick had gone?"

"There was the jug, half full, and one mug, not used, mam."

"Looks bad for Dugald, doesn't it?" said Mrs. Bradley pleasantly. "It looks as though he didn't *expect* to find anybody else up there. How much do the mugs hold?"

"Best part of three-quarters of a pint," said Tom hoarsely, "but young Dugald — "

"And the jug?"

"It's a two-pint size."

"Were you surprised to see the body thrown up on the rocks, Tom?"

Tom stared, astonished at the sudden change of ground.

"No," he said. "Of course not. The way these currents run it was bound to be like that. The chap as chucked Dick overboard was a fool."

"No. Ignorant. Murderers often are. How many times did you have to leave your bunk that night, Tom?"

"Three times, and Dugald twice and Walt twice. They got stronger stomachs than me. Sick as toads we was, all three of us."

x

"You can arrest Walt for the murder," said Mrs. Bradley, later, astonishing the Inspector by her satisfied, confident tone.

"But how do you know?" he enquired.

"Tom knew the body would be washed up on to the rocks. Therefore I suggest that Tom is innocent."

"We've thought that all along. It was rough on the old fellow we had to mix the sheep and the goats. But what about Dugald? Your point about the jug and the mug struck my men as pointing to his guilt. They thought you'd got him properly there."

"I think not. Had there been more cocoa in the jug I might agree. What Dugald did was to take up one mug only — with the idea of dividing the rather inconsiderable amount of cocoa between himself and Dick, one having the mug and the other what remained in the jug. Did you ever know a man wash up an extra utensil when he need not? *I* never did."

"I believe you. But how do you pin it on Walt? I agree you've eliminated the others, but will all this convince a jury?"

"Yes, when you've found the woman in the case — Dick's wife, I should rather imagine. Meanwhile, here is your evidence. Something had upset the men's stomachs that night — and lighthouse keepers don't have queasy insides. Each man had to leave the bunk-room from time to time during the early part of the night. You'll be able to find out what they had to eat. The point is that Walt was the cook. He could, and you'll find that he did, doctor the suppers of Dugald and Tom. He would not have doctored his own, but he made the same excuse as they did, to leave the bunk-room. What's more, I'm sure he's lying when he says he only went out once. The first time he went out he killed Dick, and the second time he tumbled the body over the gallery rail. He did not dare to risk staying away long enough to do both deeds at one time. His mistake was that he had not studied the tides. He was almost new to that lighthouse."

Rushy Glen

The majority of exuberant people sing in their baths. Laura Menzies, personal private secretary to Mrs. Lestrange Bradley, psychiatrist and private detective, always recited in hers.

On a fine, crisp morning in February at approximately eight of the clock, Laura, splashing vigorously, was proclaiming in tones which did credit to the power of her lungs William Allingham's masterpiece of fairy lore, "Up the Airy Mountain."

"Up the airy mountain, down the rushy glen, we dare not go a-hunting, for fear of Little Men," bellowed Laura. There came a knock at the door, and the voice of Mrs. Bradley's French maid followed it.

"Madame would like to see you very soon, please.

"There has been a strange accident, Mademoiselle, and Madame is puzzled."

"Murder?"

"It is Madame who thinks so."

"Cheers."

"She wishes to know if she shall take steps."

"Tell her to expect me in a couple of ticks."

Breakfast in winter at Mrs. Bradley's country house was usually at nine, but when Laura got downstairs at twenty past eight she found her employer already seated at table. Mrs. Bradley was making rapid hieroglyphics in a small notebook.

"Help yourself to a great deal of breakfast and eat while I unfold my tale," said Mrs. Bradley. "When I have done, and you are ready, we are going to Reedglen Common. A man was found dead there this morning.

"He was in hunting costume and must have had a bad fall. At least, that is what we are meant to believe. His skull was crushed."

"He fell on a rock, then, I take it? It's pretty treacherous through there. But how do *you* come into it?"

"I was called upon, as the nearest doctor. The body is in Stinchester mortuary. There will be an inquest, of course, and I shall be called upon to give evidence.

"The trouble is that I cannot believe the death was accidental. You see, there did not happen to be any rocks or stones nearby, and it seemed to me that the man should have broken his neck on ground like that, instead of smashing in the top of his head.

"He had been wearing one of those hunting bowlers too — the reinforced kind such as I have seen worn in the Cotswold country. It was still on his head, and one would have thought it would act as a crash helmet."

"Is the dead man somebody you know?"

"Not at all well, although I have met him on the hunting field. He is Mr. Thomas Cutting, of Hornbeams Farm."

"Oh? A bit of a beauty, wasn't he, by all accounts? Probably a man to have made enemies."

"There seems to have been some gossip. He is not a local man, and I think there were discontented people when he rented the farm. Some think that Mr. William Cashell, who wanted it for his son Gerald, should have had it."

"And Gerald has since become a bad hat," said Laura, thoughtfully. "Isn't that the size of it? Haunts pubs, and is on the shady side of bookmaking — that sort of thing."

"I have heard as much."

"Then there's Remington, at Long Acres," Laura continued. "He hasn't been too pleased with Cutting since that mare of his had to be shot after Cutting's bull got loose and savaged it.

"I know Cutting had to pay up and that Remington stuck him for the price, but he was very fond of that mare, and had a lot to say in the local about what he'd do to Cutting one of these days. You don't think he's carried out his threat?"

"I propose to keep an entirely open mind, child."

×

Reedglen Common was about three miles from Mrs. Bradley's house. The cowman who had discovered the body had come on his bicycle, and Mrs. Bradley had taken him back in her car, but now she and Laura walked the distance, making a detour which brought them on to the road from the dead man's farm, which was less than two miles from the common.

"Now, keep your eyes open," said Mrs. Bradley. "I saw that body at just after half-past seven. The man had been dead between six and eight hours."

"Then he was riding in the dark when it happened!"

"That is the inference. I have informed the police, of course, and they will investigate."

"By the way, what happened to the horse?" asked Laura.

"I have no idea. I asked the man (who brought the news) whether he had seen it. It probably galloped off home, but that we can find out later.

"Now here is where he would have turned off to get to the common. Look very carefully for fresh hoof-prints. It rained last evening and the ground is still beautifully damp."

"Did you find much trampling around where the body was lying?"

"Yes, of one horse."

"Well, that's all we need, isn't it? — Oh, I see what you mean! The murderer might also have been on horseback! That is, if it *was* murder."

"Either that, or, of course, he might have persuaded Mr. Cutting to dismount."

"I still can't see why he was able to get up behind him and clout him over the head like that, though. Can you? Besides, Mr. Cutting is such a big man. I shouldn't think many people would be tall enough to get in a blow like that, unless — "

"Yes?" said Mrs. Bradley encouragingly.

"It's probably a silly idea, but could it be that Cutting, in spite of the way he was dressed, was *not* on horseback, but that the murderer was? You said one horse, you know."

"Continue."

"Well, I wondered — I mean, suppose you were wearing this reinforced hunting bowler and I rode up and knocked it off your head and — no, I can see for myself that's silly. The whole point about hunting hats is that they're built *not* to come off at all easily. You couldn't knock his hat off with one hand and cosh him with the other, could you?"

"It might be possible, but it is hardly probably, I think; but pray continue your valuable observations, remembering that the hat was still on when the body was found."

"You're pulling my leg," said Laura, with her enchanting grin. Mrs. Bradley solemnly shook her head.

"Your reasoning is a little obscure," she said, "and yet, as the setting sun to the rising moon, you shed considerable light."

"Proceed, moon," said Laura cheekily.

"I will. And, like the moon (inconstant, according to the poets), I am going to change my mind. When we have scouted round I shall make for Hornbeam's Farm."

"Mr. Cutting's, do you mean?"

"Exactly so."

×

A smart sergeant came up, saluted, said that he had orders to give Mrs. Bradley every facility, and left them to their own devices. Mrs. Bradley walked up to a mackintosh sheet which covered part of the wild and tussocky ground. She and Laura carefully peeled it back. It covered the spot where the body had been found.

"But there's no blood anywhere!" cried Laura. "Wouldn't a crushed skull bleed? It must mean — "

"Yes?"

"Well, it must mean that he wasn't killed where he was found!"

"Elementary, my dear Watson," said Mrs. Bradley.

"Yet here are the hoof-marks, plenty of them," said Laura; and she pointed to where the reedy tufts had been trampled and churned. Mrs. Bradley nodded and led the way towards the farm.

"Go on," she said. "Tell me more."

"No can do. What's this single-line wheel-track we're following? Made by a wheelbarrow ... or am I wrong?"

"I trust a child. Ah, there's the farmhouse."

They lost the single wheel-track at the edge of a little copse. The path they were following picked up a cattle drive, and the broader track was trampled and thick with mire.

"You mean Mr. Cutting was killed in his own house and the body taken to the common in a wheelbarrow, don't you?" said Laura.

"Yes, I do. I am going to ask about hats when we get to the farm though. That hat had been placed on the dead man's head after he was killed," said Mrs. Bradley, "a point which will not have escaped the notice of the police.

"Now for the stableman, to ask, not whether a horse is missing, but *which* horse. It may give us a pointer, I think."

The stableman was rather cross with them.

"The police has been here for an hour or more," he protested. "Yes, there *is* an 'oss missing. It's Firelight, our best mare. Took fright when she threw the master, I reckon, and bolted. She've got real blue blood in her, that mare have, and I reckon she's in Warwickshire by now."

"I thought she was in foal," said Laura. "Someone said so, down in the village. Firelight, I'm sure, was the name."

"Well," said the stableman, staring, "so she be, and likely to throw the colt at any minute. This'll be the end of 'er, this will."

"Wasn't it curious, then, that your master chose her for a risky ride in the dark?" Mrs. Bradley inquired, giving Laura a surreptitious pat on the back.

The stableman scratched his head.

"Come to think on it," he said, "I reckon that's about right. Still p'raps you didn't know the master. Nothing to hold or to bind when his temper was on him.

"And when old Cashell come blowin' round 'ere last night with a song about the lease, well, the master, 'e proper got it up the nose, as you might say."

"Did they quarrel?"

"Now, look you 'ere — they may 'ave, or they may 'ave not. The master paid me good money, and that's the reason I stopped on (and the only reason), but Mr. Cashell, he's a gentleman, he is, and I ain't saying owt to get him into trouble."

"When did your master buy his new hunting hat?"

"Search me! What's he want with a new hat? His pork-pie for market, and his topper when he went huntin' — only I took that to be reblocked, would a-been day before yesterday — and 'is trilby for church. What more would he want with 'ats?"

"What breeches was your master wearing yesterday?"

"He didn't 'ave his breeches on yesterday. He wore his velveteens," said the stableman, staring.

"Did the police ask you that?"

"No, they didn't."

"I wish to see these velveteens."

"Nothing to do with me. They'll be in his room."

"Right. We'll go up to the house. Thank you very much for your trouble."

"Eh? Oh, much obliged, I'm sure. Ask for Mrs. Nuckett up at the 'ouse. She's took over everything since the poor missus pegged out, five years ago, and a rare good sort she be."

×

Mrs. Nuckett was not inclined to be helpful.

"She's scared," muttered Laura, when the housekeeper had been persuaded to go upstairs for the velveteens. "Do you think she did it?"

"Unlikely, child, I feel. A woman is seldom handy with a cosh, especially a woman past middle-age. I think she's worried about the police visit, that's all. But here come the velveteens, to tell us, I hope, their story."

She took them from the housekeeper, diligently searched the pockets, and found nothing.

"Thank you," said Mrs. Bradley, handing the garments back. "Would you mind telling me whether Mr. Cutting had any callers last night after you had gone up to bed?"

The woman looked thoroughly alarmed.

"There was a knock at the door as soon as I'd put my lamp out," she replied, "but I don't know who it was that came."

"Your master's murderers," said Mrs. Bradley calmly. "At what time did the older Mr. Cashell leave?"

"Just after nine. I took the master his supper in as soon as Cashell had gone."

"Did your master seem angry or upset?"

"No. He was laughing, and pleased with himself. He said to me as how he'd told Cashell, once and for all, what he thought of his good-for-nothing son. It done him good to get it off his chest, he said."

×

"I can't see how you knew," said Laura, later, when young Gerald Cashell had been arrested for the murder, and his father and Farmer Remington as accessories after the crime. "What put you on to the truth?"

"The mare in foal," Mrs. Bradley replied, "and the hunting bowler, and the obvious fact that no one man could have carried out this particular crime without help."

"Do tell me, please."

"It was this way: first, there was no blood, as both you and the police observed, where the dead man's body was found. That was the most valuable clue of all.

"Then there was the question of the hat. You see, if the inference were to be that Mr. Cutting, who never went out without a hat, had met his death by a fall from a horse, he had to be dressed for the part.

"All that was necessary was for the murderer to change Mr. Cutting's velveteens for some riding breeches. Easy enough.

"Then came the question of a hat. What the murderer did not know was that the topper had been sent to be reblocked.

"Mr. Cutting, you see, was rather a dressy man. He possessed a pork-pie hat for market and a trilby for church, but, to the murderer, neither the pork-pie nor the trilby seemed quite the thing, as Mr. Cutting was particular in these matters.

"The only thing to do was to supply him with a suitable hat, and, to cut a long story short, that hat has been traced by the police to the Cashells. It belonged to young Gerald Cashell.

"Fortunately, or so the murderer though, it was a pretty good fit."

"I can see that Gerald Cashell had to have help in getting the body out of the house and on to the wheelbarrow, and that that could involve his father," said Laura slowly, "but how does Mr. Remington come into it?"

"*You* settled Remington's hash. No countryman worthy the name would elect to take a dangerous ride at night on a mare which might at any time drop her foal, yet hoof-prints had to be provided at the scene of the death.

"Now Remington's own mare had been killed (so he would see it) by Cutting's bull. What more fitting, then, than when the Cashells enlisted his aid to bring a horse to the glen, Remington should choose the blood mare? He even rode her to where the body lay. It had been deposited there by the Cashells using the wheelbarrow.

x

"Of course, Remington may not have been told the whole truth about the murder. That remains to be seen, but the choice of the mare in foal involves him."

"I'm glad the mare was found unharmed, anyhow," said Laura. "And the foal is a beauty. I'd like to buy it. In fact, I think I must."

"I do not advise that, child," said Mrs. Bradley, with her grim cackle. "For seven years you might never see it again! It was born in a fairy ring!"

Juniper Gammon

You mean Jupiter Gammon, said I. The pig-keeper shook his head.

Juniper Gammon, he repeated. And a rare good old boar that he, too. Named after his grandfather, that be. There's a tale how his granddad came by the name that you'd find it interesting.

I accepted the hint, and, after a last admiring look at the fine old boar — a Tamworth he was — rather an unusual pig in that district — I led the pig-keeper pub-wards.

It were all on account of Mrs. Doubleday, the sexagenarian began. Her and her son, they kept the village shop in them days — afore the war it were — and the young feller always on the fidget to get a move up to London.

"I could get on better there," he say, "but mam, her won't come along."

"Then go by yourself," I say.

"Ah, but, then, if I do, mam, she'll leave shop to bor Tom."

This Tom was own cousin to the family, and lodged further on in the village, and I could understand the lad's feelings, particular when his mother sold up the shop of a sudden — all of a queer do us thought it — and bought a litter o' pigs, and some hens and a cock with the money. Well, what the old lady do to the pigs us don't know, but there's no doubt they prosper pretty fairly. How she do it none of us know, but it's rarely like gardening, I reckon. Some can grow plants and crops in any sort of soil and some never will.

Well, the young chap, Johnnie his name was, that didn't seem to take to the pigs no more than he did to the shop.

"I want to be off, mam," he say. "I want to try my hand at a garage in London town."

So one fine day he up and go, and, sure enough, before the week was out, Tom come to live with his auntie and go to work tending the garden.

I said his auntie had a hand with the stock; well, the same this bor Tom with the garden.

Quite a picture it were, till one day bor Johnnie come home. Hadn't made much success in London, it seem.

"Get out of it," that say to bor Tom. "Who want you here?"

So Tom, that up with his fists, and they fight it out to see if the better man win. Johnnie win. Seem he had a hard time in London, and Tom, that get soft with easy living.

×

When Johnnie had turned Tom out, he set to work and he pull up every plant in the garden.

Then he let the pigs on to the garden.

His poor mam, that don't know what to do. That beg him to stop this evil work and to go away, but that say he won't.

"Then I'll put the police on you, Johnnie," say his mam. "I give you a week to put the pigs back and put all my garden to rights, and then you can clear yourself off and I'll have bor Tom back to live here."

But before to-morrow was a week, Johnnie he lay down dead. It was after a hot supper of pork. Not too good a time for pork, the middle of June. Johnnie go down to the pub when supper was over and have a few beers, and must have come back then to try conclusions with the boar.

The boar — Juniper Gammon, granddad of the Tamworth you've just been lately seeing — he were tougher a lot than bor Tom, and next morning, when Tom come creeping back to help put the garden to rights (for he couldn't bear to leave it like it was), he found Johnnie dead in the sty, and the blood hardly showing on Juniper Gammon's sandy snout.

Course, there had to be an inquest, and crowner's verdict were clear. Death by misadventure savaged by a boar. And then, Mrs. Doubleday's pigs, they begin to die.

×

Well, we had a visitor in the village that summer, an elderly sort of old maw by the name of Bradley. Interest her strangely, that death did. Look at it from all angles, like an old politician, that did, and then that begin to ask question.

"Savaged by a boar?" she say. "What boar? And for why was he savaged by a boar?"

Us told her what boar, but nothing would content her but to be introduced, you might say, to Juniper Gammon in person.

"So this boar savage him?" say the old maw. "He's a very fine pig," that say. "My nephew keep pigs down in Oxfordshire."

×

So us talk pig for a long time, looking at Juniper Gammon (named Surlingham Gammon that was then), and bit by bit the tale come out about bor Johnnie and his mam and bor Tom.

"I was present at the inquest," say the old maw. "That seem as if Johnnie Doubleday climb over into boar's pen. Didn't that know the danger? And a Tamworth at that? Proud, that always is, a Tamworth boar."

Right she were there.

Anyway, we explain to her how queer that seem that bor Johnnie should venture into the pen of a boar, seeing that seemingly he were too frit even to scratch a little pig's back with the end of a long stick.

"And the other pigs died?" her say thoughtful-like.

"The main of them. More than Mrs. Doubleday want to lose, and bor Johnnie, that take them away, but Juniper Gammon and three sows that hadn't been turned out by Johnnie in his temper, they replace them with very fine litters.

"Come you over here, mam, and you can see them." So say I to her.

But that prefer to linger by Juniper Gammon.

×

"I wonder Mrs. Doubleday doesn't want to get rid of this fellow," that say, "seeing that he savage her son."

"That do, now her pigs are replaced," say I, "and from to-morrow, the boar belong to me."

We see very little of the old maw after that. That go poking around the woods and the fields, and that ask for Tom to be her guide. Then we get a shock in the village. It seem someone has made some trouble, and bor Johnnie to be dug out of his grave.

Nobody care for that idea. Rector, at first, that forbid it. Bor Johnnie were properly buried in our own churchyard, and our churchyard is holy ground and not to be disturbed except by the sexton.

But a police order silence rector, and in the dead of the night there's the sound of falling spades, and up come coffin with bor Johnnie inside, and the doctors go to their work on his mortal remains.

×

Well, poor old Mrs. Doubleday, that have been looking poorly ever since Johnnie's death, and the shock of having him dug up and cut to pieces by the doctors, and all the questions the police come round to ask her, they prove too much for the poor old maw.

That lay down and sicken, and that die.

The doctors and policemen take their time, and after her funeral her will was read out, and it seem she leave everything she have to a pig-breeders' club over Swaffham way.

Bor Tom, that didn't seem surprised.

"That wouldn't leave it to Johnnie, but, if not to Johnnie, then that wouldn't leave it to me. No expectations there," he tell everyone.

Farmer, that tell him keep the cottage, and that continue to set the garden to rights and that plant it again, and that go back to working for farmer and do pretty fairly.

×

Well, that do pretty fairly until the old maw, Mrs. Bradley, come round and begin asking questions. All in the papers, afterwards, that was, so we know what she go round and say.

That ask Tom who else ate the hot pork supper the night Johnnie died, and Tom, that say nobody did. Mrs. Doubleday, that didn't fancy hot pork before going to bed, and have cooked it to eat cold, and Tom himself was too frit of Johnnie, after the fight they'd had, to come near the place for his meals.

"And did she eat it cold the next day?" the old maw want to know. That seem she had not; too upset at Johnnie's death to take anything more than bread and butter and a pot or two of strong tea. So cold pork go bad and get thrown away before anyone else so much as touch it.

×

Then the old maw get out of Tom how Johnnie had come into the pub and had a few beers, and Tom had kept out of his way, but help him home when the pork and the beers made Johnnie begin to feel badly.

Then the police arrest Tom for murder, and accuse him of poisoning his cousin and pitching him into the sty.

But the old maw, that say wait. That advise Tom to tell the police where he buried Mrs. Doubleday's dead pigs. And every pig that died was full up with poison to the brim. What poison? Foxglove, of course.

When Johnnie let out the young pigs they eat up all they can find in poor Tom's garden.

Tom deny that on the way home from the pub Johnnie fall down dead, and he deny he was frittened of being found by night with a dead man he fight with and lose to. He deny he pitched Johnnie into the sty to make it look as if the boar savaged him.

But the truth of it we never will know, whether Mrs. Doubleday know the pig she gave Johnnie hot for his supper that evening had ate of the foxgloves or not."

"But why Juniper Gammon?" I enquired.

"Well, we never had much to talk about in our village, and us wanted something to remember Johnnie by. It wouldn't have been decent to call the boar Foxglove, would it? But folks around these parts say juniper would poison you, too."

Manor Park

At the end of our road is a park which used to belong to a nobleman. He sold the property to the local council in 1934, and the council, rather surprisingly, did nothing much to alter the general set-up. They put a few more ducks on the lake, made the house a show-place — it has some rather good ceilings and a seventeenth-century staircase — put down a couple of bowling greens, and otherwise left well alone.

I have a brother named Bob of whom I'm more than ordinarily fond. Bob is a schoolmaster and just before last summer holidays he had a showdown with another master named Baluster. It wasn't the only row Baluster had that term, but it was the silliest. It began as an argument about the composition of the school first eleven, Baluster standing out for a boy called Bowey, a batsman, Bob inclining towards a boy named Cartwright, a bowler. Believe it or not, Baluster and Bob came to blows, and the Head was called in and was caustic. He himself picked Bowey, and the school team won. Baluster was rather insufferable as a result, but Bob ignored him.

The rest of the staff didn't care much about him, either. Jones had been called a something Welshman; Taylor had been called over the coals by the Head for mislaying a set of geography text-books and they had subsequently turned up in Baluster's cupboard, having been "borrowed" while Taylor was out with his boys on a school journey; and Vort, a brilliant young Jew very popular with the boys, had lost the affections of Irene, the headmaster's secretary, when Baluster poached on the preserves and secured her for himself.

Well, on the Thursday after the cricket match, the park-keeper, who had two rooms at the top of the mansion and acted as caretaker there, sent to the school to say that boys had been getting into the park after dark and lighting fires and doing a lot of damage. Baluster was sent along to investigate, but, of course, there was nothing to show that it was boys from the school; it might just as well have been a tramp or some town hooligans, and the Head said that, in the absence of other evidence, he was prepared to question his boys but not necessarily to blame them.

The boys naturally denied all knowledge of the damage, the masters were asked to keep their ears open, the worst of the school gangs were paraded and solemnly warned, and that was that.

At the end of term Bob brought another master home with him, a fellow named Coombes. They'd got a silly stunt on. You see, there was a ghost attached to the old house in the park, and these fellows argued that if boys could get into the park at night, so could they. There had been no more complaints of damage and the whole thing had died down. This was just as well, for the park-keeper was having his holiday and would be replaced for a week by a rather gormless son-in-law called Bitters, who wouldn't even live in the house but in a small lodge at the park gates.

On Friday night, therefore, Bob and Coombes set out to find their way into the park. They'd explored a bit during daylight and had discovered that along the riverside boundary some enterprising lads had managed to force a couple of iron railings sufficiently far apart to enable a thinnish person to squeeze through.

It was a glorious night. The moon shone on the huge cedar tree in the park and turned all the grass silver-green and picked out the grim old house. What it didn't pick out was the dead body of Baluster. Bob fell over that as he ducked in under the branches of the great old cedar as the shortest cut to the house. Bob had stumbled on to the feet of the corpse which were only just in shadow.

At first, of course, all Bob knew was that he'd stumbled over somebody lying there underneath the tree, and he couldn't think at first why the fellow didn't wake up and curse him. He called to Coombes that he thought it was a tramp who'd been taken bad. He hadn't brought a torch with him. It hadn't seemed worth while, with the moon so bright. Coombes, however, had a torch and switched it on.

"Good God!" he said. "It's Baluster!" He was lying flat on his face with his head bashed in, and the thing which had done the job was lying there close to the body — a cricket bat, looking messy and very nasty on the rounded back of the blade.

"Better not touch that!" said Bob; but Coombes had already picked it up and had carried it into the moonlight.

"It's Jones's bat!" he said. "Better take it along to the police station and make a report. We don't want the murderer coming back and removing it. He may still be in the park, for all we know."

Not a pleasant thought at midnight. Coombes kept firm hold of the bat, only giving it up to Bob when he had to crawl through the fence. Bob took it with his handkerchief round his hand, but Coombes said he didn't think the binding on the handle would take any fingerprints whatsoever. They debated the point, walking along the river bank to the town. It made something impersonal to talk about.

The police were not very pleased, and took them both back to the park to save time in finding the body — or so they said. They knocked up Bitters in the lodge to unlock the gates, and it took a long time to persuade him to get out of bed. He thought they were a gang of louts at first.

The police questioned him closely, and the police surgeon soon arrived. There was no doubt that Baluster had died between ten and twelve o'clock. The park was closed at nine-thirty, so the murderer, whoever he was, must have nipped in after hours, or stayed in after closing time.

Next day, of course, Jones was questioned about his bat. He told the police — and could prove it easily enough — that he was going to Italy for his holiday and would have no use for the bat. He had left it at school in the stock-cupboard. Anybody on the staff and any number of boys could have known this. He didn't like Baluster much, but that would apply to half the staff — that they didn't like Baluster, I mean. It certainly applied to Bob, and probably even more to Jones and Vort, although Vort, not given to brooding, had soon got himself another girl.

The police were not inclined to suspect Jones. Their argument, for what it was worth, was that a reasonably intelligent man would not have used to commit the murder a bat with his own name on it. This seemed unanswerable, unless (as Bob pointed out to me in private), Jones's intelligence was such that he would have foreseen the way that particular cat would jump and, with great boldness, had made allowance for it.

Anyway, the staff were all rounded up and their alibis checked. At home we were each called upon, separately, to declare at what time Bob and Coombes had left the house. As they had reported the murder at the police station before they returned home, that end could be checked by the police themselves.

The inspector admitted that he did not really suspect either of them, as it was rather fantastic to suppose that they would have admitted to having been in the park that night if they had committed the murder.

The handle of the bat gave no help and the contents of Baluster's pockets gave no help either. There was only one surprising thing in the inventory: that was a complete bunch of the school keys, showing that Baluster himself could have got into the stock-cupboard and helped himself to Jones's bat. As he could scarcely have committed suicide by striking himself on the back of the head with it, however, this did not seem to help the enquiry at all. There was no doubt that he had been killed where the body was found. That much was easily established by the police. He had been struck with considerable force and had been left lying exactly where he fell. It was all no end of a mystery.

The alibis of the staff seemed pretty sound. The head master had caught the night express to Fishguard on breaking-up day. Jones's alibi, supported by his landlady, was that he had spent the evening packing and then had listened to the wireless in her sitting-room until the Home Service closed down at eleven-three. Bob and Coombes supported one another, and Coombes, a very easy-going chap, had never quarreled with Baluster. Taylor, the quiet Scot, had gone up to bed with his wife at just past eleven, and had thrown some water at a cat at just before midnight. The cat couldn't swear to this, but the neighbours could. His house was six miles from the park, he had no car and was not on a bus route.

Vort had spent the evening at the International Horse Show at White City. At a quarter-past eleven he was still there, and had a couple of girls and a Jewish friend to swear to this. Manley, another member of the staff had already gone on holiday. He was brought back, but there was no doubt he had caught a seven-o'clock train for the north of England. He could prove this, and was completely exonerated. And so it went on.

The answer seemed to be a lemon, and no arrest has been made. I'm wondering how long I ought to keep quiet. So long as Bob isn't accused, I don't think I'll bother to say anything, although, if she was silly enough to give up a good boy like Vort for a so-and-so like Baluster, and then get scared of Baluster's little ways, she takes what's coming to her, so far as I'm concerned. But women do stick by women, whatever men may think, and I'll stick by her as long as I can. You see, it *must* have been the school secretary. She's the only person who fulfils all the conditions, and the police obviously have never thought of her.

What easier, after all, than to get a third set of school keys made? She'd have a bunch in her possession, naturally, and the Head would have a similar bunch. She decides to kill Baluster, whose behaviour, as a lover, has become frighteningly embarrassing. She'd get the third set of keys made, so that she need not tell anybody that her own were mislaid, then she'd unlock the stock-cupboard, get out Jones's bat — it's a golden rule never to use anything of your own for a murder — keep the assignation she'd already made with Baluster in the park, clout him with the bat before he'd realise what was coming to him, put the new bunch of keys in his pocket to confuse the issue (which it has!) leave the bat where she'd dropped it, and go off home.

I don't believe, you see, that any *man* would have used the wrong side of a bat; that's one thing. And, anyway, it wouldn't be a man that Baluster was meeting under that heavily shadowed old tree.

The Jar of Ginger

"But you would have to be certain," said Jaffrick, "that the person you wanted to murder would eat the whole lot. I mean, look at the risk otherwise. Why, you might even eat the wrong piece yourself."

We were young then. We called ourselves *The Society of Thugs* and the only rule for admission to membership was that you should describe to the club a method for murdering your nearest and dearest. We interpreted this heading widely. It could be held that *nearest* and *dearest* need not be synonymous terms. For instance, Withers had given a perfectly good and very interesting account of how he could murder his landlady, and P. J. Smith had described a method for murdering himself. In the one case the operative word was *nearest* and in the other case *dearest*, P. J. Smith holding (against no particular opposition) that he was the dearest person known to himself. For one thing he contended that he was of more expense to himself than anybody else was (he was a bachelor, of course), and he confessed also that he preferred himself and his own company even to us and ours.

It was a man called Chart who had drawn the remark from Jaffrick. Chart was not known personally to any of us. He had rolled up in company with Bellew, but Bellew had only run into him that evening in a bar, and as Chart (admittedly slightly stewed when they arrived) had stood him a drink because he said he liked his face, Bellew had brought him along after telling him the terms of membership.

He was a good deal older than the rest of us. Forty-five, I should say, and his story of how he could murder his wife was interesting enough in a sense, but, as Jaffrick argued, the method he described could not be guaranteed to work. The risk to the murderer was as great as to the intended victim.

"Ah, but after a time you wouldn't put the *whole* jar of ginger on the table," said Chart. "Perhaps I ought to make that bit a little clearer. By the way, my wife is dead, so my choice of her as my victim no longer has any real significance. I shouldn't like you gentlemen to think that my selection of somebody I could murder was in questionable taste. Yes, well, you see, you'd buy the pot of ginger ... one of those handsome, decorated, Chinese things, you know ... as a present to the house around

Christmas time. You'd buy the biggest and most beautiful pot you could afford, because the more ginger you had to play about with, the easier your task would be and the greater its chance of success.

"Well, at first you would dig for your ginger, and the wife would dig for hers. This would go on for quite some time, the ginger, of course, innocent stuff, gradually getting lower and the action of digging for it stickier.

"One point that I must emphasise is that for the successful carrying out of your plan you would need to keep the pot of ginger firmly under your own control. This could be done by insisting, with humorous gallantry, that you always place it upon the table yourself.

" 'No, it's *my* present to the house,' you would laughingly say, looking at it affectionately as it stood in its celestial glory on the sideboard. 'Nobody else need even dust it! I'll see to all that!' Of course, if you had any sense, you wouldn't make it the first present to the house that you had ever bought. If one proposes to murder one's nearest and dearest, one leads up to it by degrees. Even three years is not too long to wait. There is no point in bungling the job, let alone spoiling the ship for a ha'porth of tar.

"Well, when the ginger in the jar was low enough to make spearing it out a messy, sticky business, you would introduce your next little move. You would bring home a very small, expensive, cut-glass dish ... something about the size of a domestic ash-tray. In fact, a really lovely ash-tray about three to four inches across would do as well as anything else.

" 'Look, darling,' you would say. 'For our lovely ginger! And when we've finished the ginger we've got a perfectly good ash-tray. My next present to the house had better be some super-Turkish or Egyptian.' "

"But I can't see a woman swallowing all this, you know," said Jaffrick. "I mean, by the time you'd got to this stage you'd have had disagreements and a good many quarrels. I mean, she would tend to suspect your *bona fides* and so forth, wouldn't she?"

"That would depend upon how much you hated her," replied Chart. "If it was only the ordinary give and take of the average married couple, she would naturally suspect your good intentions. She would take it for granted that you were covering up some peccadillo of your own by bringing back presents for the house. But a real, honest, devilish, implacable hatred, that's quite a different matter. You would disguise that as long as ever you could, because you would know that sooner or later it would mean either murder or divorce, and divorce is so confoundedly expensive."

We all gloomily agreed. We were young, as I said, and all bachelors. It takes a bachelor to be ideally (as it were) gloomy and profound about marriage.

"Go on about the ginger," said Bellew, for our guest showed signs of dropping off to sleep. "The trouble, as I see it, would not be to disguise your hatred — any competent hater could do that! — but to make perfectly certain, ash-tray or no ash-tray, that you didn't pick the wrong piece of ginger yourself."

"Simplicity itself," said P. J. Smith. "You'd stick a pin in the poisoned lump and then chew carefully."

We all disputed this, an ordinarily silent bloke called Carruthers and myself holding that the danger of swallowing or being pricked by the pin would be almost equal to the danger of swallowing the lethal dose in the piece of ginger, and, further, that if the victim struck on the pin she would throw the rest of the ginger away.

"Pins!" said P. J. Smith. "Oh no! Who on earth worries about pins? Stuck them deeply into chaps at school, and chaps at school stuck them deeply into me. Nothing to it. Nobody cares about pins!"

Carruthers and I said that we did, and the pin and anti-pin argument lasted the club for half an hour and tended to embrace such subjects as canteen meals and the recent bus strike. It then passed lightly over films, the scenery around the Matterhorn and yachting on the Norfolk Broads. In fact, Rowbotham, our president, had to call the meeting to order.

"Will somebody move," he said plaintively, "that the prospective candidate be allowed to continue his exposition?"

Half a dozen of us who were losing the argument immediately accommodated him, and Chart resumed his remarks.

"You see," he said, when we had woken him up, "one would only put out four pieces of ginger each time on the small glass dish."

"Three-to-one chance," said Bellew.

"Granted," said Chart, "and your remarks about pins have interested me deeply. Nevertheless, there would be one infallible rule. You yourself would always choose your piece of ginger first. This would reduce the odds, of course, but, in my view, unnecessarily. There would always be a slight element of chance or risk, but the wise man would slice off the end of the noxious piece of ginger so that he could recognise it. The technique is really very simple. One would spear an innocuous piece of ginger, leaving three other pieces on the dish. It might be that the party of the second part would pick the piece with the strychnine in it straight away. If not, there would be only two pieces left, and a wise murderer would give his victim the choice of these, and not attempt to encourage her to eat both."

"I can't see that," said Bellew. P. J. Smith said that of course he could. If the victim picked the non-poisonous piece it would be simplicity itself to say that one did not want any more and leave it at that. Other members disputed this. It would look very fishy, they said to leave a piece on the dish if one was not in the habit of doing this. And what of the ill-manners of helping oneself first? they enquired.

Chart, looking crestfallen, agreed.

"Besides, what would you do with the fatal piece?" asked Bellew, pressing home his advantage. "You could hardly put it back into the jar, and you'd not want to throw it away and doctor up another piece, would you?"

P. J. Smith argued that to throw it away would be the only thing to do. He contended, however, that as strychnine is not readily purchasable, one would have to hope for the best. One could not go on indefinitely impregnating pieces of ginger with poison in the hope that at some point the intended victim would choose the right chunk and consume it.

"There's the mathematical odds to consider," said Carruthers. "The permutations and combinations even of so small a number as four must be quite exhilarating."

As he was an accountant by profession, we gave him best over that.

"But do go on, Mr. Chart," said Bellew. "After all, this is your story, and, so far, I'm bound to tell you that you have my vote of membership. I don't think your scheme would work, but there are possibilities in it."

Chart said that he was obliged to him, and the rest of us politely applauded.

"You see," he said, "actually it's quite easy. A person who likes ginger in syrup would be fond of mango chutney. One would, therefore, slip the poisoned piece of ginger into the mango chutney, where it would be inconspicuous, I think, and when the chutney came on the table one would avoid that particular piece. Sooner or later, surely, the intended victim would be bound to choose it, and — hey presto! — one would be a widower without trouble or risk."

"I don't know about risk," said a man named Denison. "The symptoms of poisoning by strychnine are rather obvious, aren't they?"

"But it need not be strychnine," said P. J. Smith. "A lethal quantity of arsenic would be just as good, and the symptoms of arsenical poisoning are not easily distinguished from those of acute indigestion. I move that we accept Mr. Chart's account, substituting arsenic for strychnine."

We all voted in favour of this amendment except Carruthers, who said that the introduction of a piece of China ginger into a mango chutney would arouse doubt and suspicion in the mind of the intended victim. In mango chutney, he contended, one did not expect to find any kind of ginger but the long, narrow, hairy kind, unsweetened and as hot as hell, which forms part of the contents of any respectable jar.

This statement called for more beer and considerably more argument. As it was getting late, even for us, Bellew suggested that Mr. Chart be allowed to conclude his exposition, as the caretaker would be wanting to close the premises. We did not pay enough rent, he pointed out, to be in a position to take too many liberties.

This seemed common sense. Chart begged our pardon (rather thickly) for keeping us out of bed, and said that really he had finished what he had to say. We began to collect the tankards and glasses, but P. J. Smith said that he would like to ask the new member a question.

"I can see," he said, "that ginger, either in syrup or in a chutney, would be almost a perfect vehicle for poison, but what if the subject didn't like it?"

"Oh, but she did," said Chart. "She absolutely loved it, don't you see."

The Knife

Well, I don't see why you should caution me, I'm sure. Anybody would think I might not be telling the truth. It was all on account of the Gurkha knife.

What do they call it? I couldn't tell you. It's a great, big, keen-edged thing. Oh, I mean a kukri, do I? Well, you'd know.

All I know is I had to keep on haggling for it before I bought it. Yes, it was at the seaside. One of those phony antique shops at the top of the cliff. But I thought perhaps Roger might like it for his birthday. A kukri, you say? Oh, well, I didn't know what to call it. I just saw it in the window, you know.

And you know how it is with men. A cigarette lighter, a shirt or two, a handkerchief and a tie to match, or gloves ... and you've had it. Unless you give them a book token.

Well, Roger doesn't read, except those dim sporting papers and all that, so a book token was out of it. You couldn't agree more, could you? So I thought he might like this knife thing.

We'd gone to the seaside for ten days, and the weather had been quite good. One morning we came up by the cliff-railway after bathing, and I suddenly got the idea. We'd passed the place before, of course, and I love junk ... most women do ... but there was always the cocktail before lunch to be fitted in, so I'd never actually stopped.

But this time I did stop. Roger wasn't terribly keen, so he went on to the hotel with our towels and things while I went into the shop. I said it was a junk shop, didn't I?

Well, it wasn't so much of a shop, if you know what I mean. It was one of those glass-house sort of shacks, and the stock was showing in the windows on all four sides.

The man in charge was a smart Alec all right. He came forward at once with a Chelsea china figure in one hand and an old-fashioned bread-board in the other. So I knew he was no good.

How did I know? Well, I just knew, if you know what I mean. But, to go on (if that's what you want), I hit upon this knife, but I told the man that I wouldn't be able to pay my hotel bill if he charged me what he was asking.

Anyway, after I'd been haggling each morning after bathing and directly after tea for three days, he suddenly kind of gave in. "All right," he said. "You take it. Here you are then. Twenty-five bob."

That's what had me worried. I'm not telling you what he asked me in the first place, but 25 shillings was a big drop. I'd been prepared to give 35 if I had to, so of course I bought the thing without second thought.

I took it back to the hotel, but I didn't let on to Roger, I wanted it to be a surprise. No, we haven't any children. Why do you ask me that? Oh, surprising people with presents? Yes, I see.

×

Well, about the knife. I bargained for it and I got it, and I took it back to the hotel. I hid it in the top of the wardrobe. You know these hotel wardrobes, don't you? Nobody ever looks on the top shelf. Not if he's a man, that is.

I always had to serve out Roger's ties and things. He never could find a thing for himself. I always had to cope.

Oh, you can believe that, can you? I'm surprised to hear you admit it. After all, you're a man, too, aren't you? If one can call a policeman a man. It doesn't seem to me a man's job, to bully women with all these redundant questions, but, of course, this is my first experience of the police.

I shouldn't be insulting? But why not? You're insulting me, aren't you? Having me come downstairs like this, and talking to me as though I were a murderess! Don't you think things are bad enough for me already?

We'd never got on, as you seem to know. Some people don't. I mean, look at those film stars and things. But there's a big gap ... and you'll have to admit it ... between wanting to do something desperate, such as killing your husband, and actually doing it.

No, I will not admit anything at all. Well, if you put it that way, perhaps I didn't buy the knife to give it him for a present.

No, all right, then. I didn't intend to give him the knife at all. I bought it for my own purpose and to give myself a sense of power.

Power! It's a wonderful feeling. I knew a PT instructor once, and he said that the biggest thrill he got out of his job was the sense of absolute power over other people's bodies and minds. It was like being a god, he said. Come to that, he was ...

A dangerous point of view? Yes, I know. We all know, nowadays, don't we? But that's what the world has come to, say what you like.

Primitive? Well, of course. I'm primitive. Aren't you? No? Well, perhaps women are different. All I know is that you're going to get me hanged if you can, and, after all, I've never done you any harm that I know of.

Coming back to the knife? I'm sick to death of the knife. I don't really know why I bought it. It cost more money than I wanted to spend, but it was for Roger, you see, so I didn't really grudge it, and it was ever such fun, haggling for it in that little glass-fronted shop.

Oh, I'm going back on what I've already said, am I? Well, why shouldn't I? I'm sure you're not allowed to keep on pestering me like this. You mean I said I wanted to do Roger in? Well, but I didn't do it. I may have wanted to do it, but I didn't.

My alibi? Oh, but I haven't got one. I don't need one. You see, when I got back to the hotel with the ... kukri, didn't you call it? ...

Roger was having his lunch. I thought he might have waited for me, but he was playing golf that afternoon, so I didn't really mind very much. I felt I had to create a bit, of course, and so I did. I've admitted we didn't get on, and anyway he used to be just as nasty to me if I was late. You'd know if you'd ever been married.

You've made up your minds I did it, haven't you? Well, I didn't do it. Give a guess who did? You've no right to ask me that either, have you?

No, I haven't a lawyer. I can't afford a lawyer, and that's the plain truth. We never had too much money, and until Roger's will is proved I don't really know where I stand.

No, I don't put it that you're exceeding your instructions, but there are such things as the Savage rules, you know. Personally, I still think you're bullying me. I needn't answer the questions unless I like to? Oh, that's a good one. And suppose I refuse to answer? You and your sergeant with his shorthand notebook!

×

All right, here it is, then. I took the knife to the hotel, as I told you, and hid it at the top of the wardrobe. Reason? The only reason was that I wanted it to be a surprise to Roger. There was no other reason at all.

Am I sticking to me statement? Of course I am. Did you look for finger-prints on the hilt of the knife? Of course you did, and you found mine, didn't you? I never denied handling the knife, did I?

And I suppose you found the shopkeepers' fingerprints, too? Superimposed on mine? Well, that's quite likely, isn't it? Why shouldn't they be? We both handled the thing. In fact, I should think it went backwards and forwards between us dozens and dozens of times.

Yes, I know what I'm saying. Of course I do. Why shouldn't I? I'm reasonably intelligent enough. In fact, I'm quite intelligent enough to know what you're getting at.

×

You've come to your own conclusions, have you? You're welcome to them, I must say. Trying to get my friends into trouble!

Well, naturally I got quite friendly with the man at the antique shop. Of course I did. I've got a friendly nature and I went in there quite a bit, what with bargaining for the knife and all that.

What did I do after Roger had gone out after lunch? Oh, I don't know. I just messed about, I think. Did I look at the knife again? I've no idea. I may have done.

Yes, as a matter of fact, I'm sure I did. Why shouldn't I? I'd bought it, hadn't I? Out of my own money, too, if you want to know. Yes, my winnings at bridge. There's nothing against winning money at bridge, is there? Unless you cheat, I mean.

Poker? I don't play poker. You're surprised? You flatter me. It makes a nice change. Your flattery, I mean. You've been rather horrid, so far. Gloves? Kid gloves or otherwise, I never wear the things at the seaside.

Did the antique dealer ever come up to the hotel? No, of course not. Why should he? How do I explain, then, how his fingerprints came to be superimposed on mine on the hilt of the knife?

But you can't catch me out like that. I don't attempt to explain it. Why on earth should I? The inference is that he killed poor Roger, I suppose, but that's what I've thought all day, only I had nothing to go on.

Did I what? No, I did not go back to the shop with the knife. No, I did not write Roger an anonymous letter inviting him to see what his wife was up to in the woods with the fellow from the antique shop. I deny everything. Everything, do you hear!

I don't care who saw me in the woods. I don't care what they said I was carrying. I don't care what they say was wrapped round the handle. I don't care what the police deduce from that, or anything else in this world.

I didn't do it, I tell you. I didn't do it. I didn't. I didn't. I DIDN'T!

Practical Joke

Nobody could feel sorry for Sonning. He was such a dim sort of chap. He never amounted to much, either at work or in his home.

His wife despised him, and the other chaps at the office did, too. He was unimaginative and silly and was given to practical jokes ... not very unkind ones, just rather stupid ones, that's all.

I think they were his only means of expressing himself, and the most stupid part about them was that they never really came off, except once. This sole success of his came off 100 percent.

I was lodging with the Sonnings at that time. I was the woodwork master at the local school, and the digs they offered were not at all bad; neither was the price.

I didn't mind Sonning's jokes particularly, because I soon learned to go one better.

He never would leave his wife alone, though, and this used to annoy me. She was a perfectly nice woman, and, not to put too fine a point on the matter, I fell for her.

×

I found her in tears more than once as a result of his idiotic joking, but she wouldn't let me remonstrate with him.

"You'll lose your temper. You do when you argue, you know. Then he might guess. We can't risk it. He'd have to ask you to go, and I'd rather put up with anything than lose you, Tom. You know I would."

The odd thing was that he really loved his wife. I think that's the reason she put up with all his nonsense.

×

I only once knew her to remonstrate with him.

She had had her hair done rather specially because she was going to an Old Students' dance at her college. She was going with a man who had been "up" with her ... a nice type, married and with a couple of kids. His wife was going, too, and as Sonning had turned down the invitation — to everybody's relief, I should imagine — they had invited me to make a fourth.

I saw no harm in going, as it was the other chap who had suggested it ... I stood him a couple of drinks later ... so she went off for this special hair-do and came back looking like a million dollars.

Well, what does that half-wit Sonning do but confront her with a water-pistol.

"Stand and deliver!" says he, in his usual giggling way; and with that he squirts water all over her new coiffure.

I don't know why she didn't kill him. Instead, she gave him one horrified look and then bolted upstairs. What she did to her hair I don't know, but it didn't look too bad when she came down again.

"You shouldn't have done that," I said to him. "It's such a waste of money."

"It's my money," he answered. I think she heard him, but I can't be certain. Anyway, she seemed quite herself when the other two came to call for us. Women are pretty marvelous, when all's said and done.

I'd hired a car. It turned up on time, and the last we saw of him that night was his waving hand at the front door, and the last we heard of him that night was his voice, quite honestly wishing us a jolly good time.

×

The dance is a bit blurry to me. To hold her in my arms was a lot better than the drinks we had in the buffet, although those were good, too. I don't think the other chap could make me out, and I took very good care that his wife shouldn't have that opportunity. Oh, I was discreet, all right ... except in my feelings. It was a good evening, and I made the most of it. I think the others did, too.

We got back at just after two. Sonning was in bed and fast asleep. We shared a pint bottle of beer ... at least, she had a sip or two out of my glass ... she didn't care a bit for drink of any kind. It was just to be matey. I loved her for it. She went upstairs after that, but I sat on for some long time going over the evening in my mind and hoping that Sonning hadn't been up to mischief in our absence. Still, there was no sound from upstairs, so, at about four, I went to bed.

×

The next day was a Saturday. I did not have to leave the house until ten. The boys were playing a match and I'd offered to umpire as the games master was down with influenza. Sonning, of course, left for the office at the usual time.

"Well," I said when he had gone. "Sleep all right?"

"Oh, yes, when I'd taken the holly leaves out of the bed," she answered. "I was prepared, of course, so I didn't really mind, except I was rather tired. He doesn't mean anything, you know."

This, I suppose, was in answer to my scowl.

"Did he say anything about the time we got home?"

"No. He hoped we'd enjoyed ourselves, and I said we had. He seemed ever so pleased with his joke."

She spoke drearily, and I suddenly swore that I'd break his neck for him.

"I didn't mind, except about my hair," she said. "I did want to look nice for you, Tom. He needn't have done what he did."

"I only hope he didn't rumble us," I replied.

"How do you mean?" She sounded a bit apprehensive, and her eyes looked scared. I laughed it off.

"Oh, nothing. Just a joke."

"I'm rather tired of jokes," she said.

I went off to football after that, and stayed out to lunch because I was so fed up with Sonning that I thought maybe I'd better not meet him again too soon.

I got back to an early tea, hoping he would have gone to watch the local team who were playing at home that week.

It was a bitterly cold day, and he came in just as tea was on the table. He rubbed his hands and thumped his chest and she suggested, rather to my surprise, that perhaps he'd better have some brandy in his tea to warm him up a bit.

Needless to say, he took kindly to this idea, although, in the ordinary way, the bottle was kept strictly for emergency use only.

"But you'll have to get it yourself," she said. "Even the smell of the bottle makes me feel sick, as you know."

"And the taste of the stuff makes you *be* sick," he said, with a loud silly laugh. "Go on and get it, there's a good girl. You can hold it at arm's length."

x

But she wouldn't go, so he and I both went, and I poured it out for him until he said when.

The postman knocked just then and she went to the front door. I'd finished my tea, so I followed her out.

When we got back she handed him a couple of letters, and he took a great gulp of tea and began to read them. She had a letter, too, and so had I, so we were all pretty much absorbed.

Suddenly there was a cry from her.

"Oh, you've changed the cups over! There's brandy in ... "

She didn't get a chance to finish. He gave an awful groan and fell forward over the table. The joke had gone against him at last.

×

No, I didn't marry her.

You see, knowing his stupid habits as she did, poor girl, I often wonder which of them she really meant to poison.

Our Pageant

You remember our pageant, of course — the Roman Legions supplied by the Youth Clubs, the rather remote Saxon saints portrayed by the Girl Guides, the Normans led by William the Conqueror (our Town Clerk distressed because his nose-piece pressed more heavily than the Pageant Master had intended), King John and his barons all signing Magna Charta like mad whenever they got any applause, and all the rest of it.

And did you notice the Morris Dancers? There were just the six of them. They could do Bean-Setting, Trunkies (not very well — the Capers are the difficulty there), Blue-Eyed Stranger and Laudnum Bunches. Teddy Pratt could do a Morris jig, too, rather nicely, but, unfortunately, so could Cyril Clark.

x

Women did not enter into this — rather, they should not have done, but you know how it is. Five good men and true do not make six good men and true, and so our stout-hearted Miss Galley from the Bank had to be pressed into service, and a certain Miss Johnson was to act as Jack in the Green.

Jack in the Green comes down to us from the Middle Ages. You don't have to be able to dance, you just play the fool and collect the money. It is a man's job, but we hadn't got a man to do it.

If you've ever taken part in a village pageant, you'll remember that rehearsals begin at least a month too soon.

It is not too soon, considering the amount of practice involved, and it is not too soon when one considers that scarcely ever is it possible to obtain a full rehearsal until about a week before the day. There are always unavoidable gaps because of people who've got something else important to do just when the Pageant Master needs them most. But it is too soon because of all the quarrels that begin.

x

We had the usual crop, but the most obstinate one was that between Teddy Pratt and Cyril Clark. It was a cut-throat rivalry over which of them should dance a Morris jig.

Well, week followed week, and both fellows practised for all they were worth, but still there was really nothing to choose between them.

Then a new factor entered into the situation. Pratt and Clark fell out about Miss Johnson. The girl was to impersonate Jack in the Green and go with the Morris dancers, so it mattered all the more to the two men which of them should be chosen to perform the Morris jig.

As the great day came nearer, bets were being laid at six to five on Clark for the Morris jig, eight to three that Parson St. George would fall off his horse, and ten to one that the financial result would show a deficit. (We were taking a silver collection from the crowd to defray expenses.)

Those that had betted on Clark lost their money, for the Pageant Master, having to make up his mind at last, picked Pratt. Clark, he thought, was rather small, being no bigger than Miss Johnson, the Jack in the Green.

The first intimation we had of something amiss was when a message came from the Pageant Master to say that Clark had withdrawn altogether from the Morris dancing. This put everybody concerned in a stew, because, Morris jig or not, it was a plain impossibility for five men — that is to say, four men and one woman — to perform dances intended for six.

"Well, much against our feeling of civic pride — if the word civic can be applied to a village — we had to ask a fellow called Fathing from Peascod to come in and dance sixth man.

Meanwhile the expected had happened. The rehearsals had gone on for so long that before the pageant, and before he withdrew from the dancing, Clark had had the banns cried three times and had wedded the Jack in the Green right under Pratt's nose, as you might say.

The great day came at last. The band came first, and then the procession followed. The Romans led, and the cavalcade from the Hall followed the Morris dancers, because we could not think of anything much to put in between.

It was at the end of the dance called Bean-Setting that the tragedy happened, and it happened right in the middle of the village green, just before the big tableau was due to move into place. There was a lot of noise during the All In and Call, and a bit of horseplay with Jack in the Green in the middle of it, and suddenly Pratt fell down dead, so we had no Morris jig after all.

Nobody could believe it at first, and then the police took over — not just Nimmett, but the real police from Hurstminster. Pratt had been stabbed to the heart, and the weapon had been about five inches long.

×

That was all we knew for a long time, and then they got a London chap on to it from Scotland Yard. He didn't know any of us, and that was a good thing really, because he could not be biased, although we could have told him of the bad blood between Pratt and Clark.

Suspicion would naturally have fallen on Clark if he had been one of the dancers, but, of course, he had taken himself out of it. Nevertheless, the Scotland Yard man got really inquisitive, because when he compared the prints he had got on the Morris sticks, not one of the sets fitted with prints he'd found on the weapon.

Then the Scotland Yard man noticed something else. On the end of the weapon was a loop so that it could be hitched on to a belt. He examined all the Morris-men's belts, but none of them had a hook to have taken the loop on the sword-stick.

×

The chap was very bright. He put two and two together all right. He asked Clark's wife if she had any objection to being measured round the waist. She had to say no, and a woman police officer was brought along to measure her. Then Clark was measured, and the Scotland Yard man knew he had solved his problem.

"You took her place as Jack in the Green," he said to Clark. "You're much the same height, but her waist is much smaller than yours. How comes it, then, that two distinctly different tag-holes have been used? See?" He showed Clark the rubbings on the belt where, some distance apart, it was obvious that the belt had been fastened in two entirely different places. There was a hook on it, too, where the lethal weapon had been hung. Easy to hide it, with all that greenery about him.

"And you married the girl so that, when it came to the murder you'd planned, she couldn't give evidence against you," the detective said in conclusion.

Clark's prints were on the sword-stick, of course, and that settled his hash.

Still, it spoilt our pageant, and we'd taken all those weeks to get it ready. It did seem rather a pity, and the silver collection was negligible, but that was only what we'd expected.

The Tree

Mr. Wideman's greatest mistake, he thought afterwards, was to have written to the council at all, let alone the number of times that he did write. But he had worked out his plans with considerable care, and the logic of his finished structure depended upon those letters.

The first of them was very mildly worded. The tree outside his house was growing too big, he stated. It darkened his drawing-room and spoilt the view from the front bedroom window. The Council thanked him for his letter and promised to forward it to the Highway Department.

Mr. Wideman's second letter was a little firmer in tone. What, he wanted to know, did the Council propose to do about his tree? Did they not realize that in a time of load-shedding, when the misuse of electric current was a national menace, they were compelling responsible citizens to light up at least an hour earlier than need be because of the shadows cast by enormous trees outside small houses?

x

The council thanked him, and said that the matter was under consideration, so Mr. Wideman, whose object was not only the elimination of the tree but of his neighbour, Mr. Dost, whom he suspected of stealing his runner beans by pulling them through the trellis on the back garden fence, got up a petition among the neighbours to have the tree removed, and one or two people, including Mr. Dost (with whom Mr. Wideman had taken great pains not to quarrel), reluctantly put down their names.

This petition, with a covering letter, reached the Council in due course, and they professed themselves sorry to hear that the tree now constituted itself a Nuisance.

Boys would be boys, they pointed out, and it was a pity that boys desired to obtain horse-chestnuts, and more than a pity that they should endanger Mr. Wideman's windows by heaving up pieces of wood, half-bricks and tennis balls in order to knock down the objects of this very natural desire.

The Council took leave to point out, however, that if Mr. Wideman desired to live in an Avenue instead of in a Road, he must expect the

Council to plant trees. The trees were an amenity, and if Mr. Wideman did not like trees it was up to him to move to a street in which these amenities did not exist.

Mr. Wideman showed the letter to those (including Mr. Dost) who had signed the petition. Autumn passed and the boys had all the horse-chestnuts. Then the leaves fell, and Mr. Wideman swept them blasphemously into the gutter, where a road-sweeper gathered them up and took them away.

Mr. Wideman's fourth and last letter, which got to the Town Hall on the morning of the tragedy, was his shortest and by far his most dramatic.

"There you are, you see. My neighbour has hanged himself on the beastly tree. Now will you come and cut it down!"

×

But before the tree could be cut down the police had to see both it and the hanging body. They had been brought to the scene by a young man on his way to work.

He had not much of a story to tell. He had been cycling past very early in the morning and had seen the body in the dim, grey light, had got off his bicycle to have a look, and had then gone straight to the nearest telephone box. Theh police had arrived on the scene just before the milkman had got that far upon his morning round.

The police inspector, a wily man and a level-headed one, used a fireman's ladder for his first look at the tree and the body, and then had the body cut down and taken to the mortuary. There the police surgeon made his examination and pronounced that life had been extinct in Mr. Dost for not fewer than seven hours and not more than nine.

×

"Wonder he didn't drag his head off, jumping from a height like that," he pronounced conversationally. "Didn't you say his feet were only just clear of the ground?"

"He didn't jump," said the inspector. "He didn't commit suicide, either. My guess is that a ladder was put up against that tree so that the rope could be fixed, and then that somebody brought the body out on a car, fixed the noose and drove slowly on. Whoever did it must have exercised very nice judgment, but it was only a question of mathematics, after all."

"So you think he was killed somewhere else?"

"Certain of it, and your evidence fixes the time. It must have been between eleven last night and one o'clock this morning, with the odds on the later time because of there being fewer people about.

"It's a very quiet road, but a good many of the residents have got cars so it's quite likely he had to wait before using his. On the other hand, it wasn't the sort of noise to attract attention from the neighbours. I'm going to have a word at once with the people on both sides, but I don't suppose they noticed amiss either.

×

Mr. Wideman welcomed the inspector and invited him in. "I expect you've come about Mr. Dost, poor fellow," he said. "I couldn't believe my ears when I heard the news.

"Not at all the suicide type, I should have said. I knew him well, of course. Many's the time we've had a pint together since his wife died, poor chap. I wonder whether that's what's been preying on his mind."

"I couldn't say, I'm sure, sir. But we are not at all certain that it was a suicide. You can't tell me anything helpful about his private life? Anybody likely to have wished him out of the way?"

"Good heavens, no, Inspector. Dost was a most kindly man. Inoffensive as they come, although I know very little of his private affairs. Money, and all that, I suppose you mean."

"Well, it doesn't sound as though you could help me much, sir. Do you happen to know whether Mr. Dost was at home last night?"

"Well, he must have been, mustn't he?"

"Not necessarily, sir."

"Anyhow, I'm afraid I don't know whether he was in or out."

"Do you possess a car, sir?"

"Yes."

"Would you mind if a I had a look at it?"

"Help yourself." Mr. Wideman handed the inspector a key. "I don't garage it here, of course. I hire a lock-up in Pond End Street. That's the number of the lock-up on the tag."

×

The inspector had a look at the car, but it told him nothing. He also interviewed people up and down the avenue and on both sides of it, but Mr. Wideman appeared to be in luck. Nobody had seen or heard anything untoward on the previous night.

The police enquiry continued in the usual exhaustive and careful way, and in the meantime a second petition went up to the Town Hall for the removal of the tree. It was not this time instigated by Mr. Wideman, but by others; nevertheless he had not the slightest hesitation in signing it.

After all, as he pointed out (probably quite truthfully), the tree now gave him the horrors when he thought of poor Dost hanging from it like that. Everybody agreed, and the man who was getting up the petition said, not only that, but it was attracting crowds of morbid sightseers whose presence detracted from the amenities of the neighbourhood.

When the petition reached the Council there was unanimous agreement among the councillors that the tree certainly must come down, and a minute to that effect was recorded. Eventually the tree was looped, sawn through, its roots dug up and a small square of turf laid on the resultant bare patch of ground.

Mr. Wideman was delighted. Not only had he got rid of Dost, who had stolen his beans, but of the tree, too. He almost contrived to forget the night when he had strolled round to Dost's back gate, gone up to the back door, invited him to have a chat and a drink, and "see what can be done about this tree business old man."

The inspector, plodding on with his seemingly thankless task had had dozens of interviews, had tried to trace the movements of every car in the neighbourhood, and had even been back to ask Mr. Wideman whether his car had been out that night and whether he thought it possible that anybody else could have got into this lock-up garage. The people in Pond End Street could tell him nothing, and Mr. Wideman, also blandly denying all knowledge, felt perfectly safe.

×

"I see the council have taken down that horse-chestnut tree — the suicide one," remarked a junior clerk to this mother on the day that the local paper came out with the news that Mr. Wideman's tree had been demolished.

"About time, too, the nasty thing," said his mother. "When it comes to people hanging themselves — "

"Lord!" said the young man, suddenly. "That's a funny thing. And I've only just thought of it!"

Without enlightening his mother, he went straight out to the nearest telephone box and rang up the police. He was invited to step round to the station if he had anything to impart concerning the death of Mr. Dost. The inspector had him sent to the office and gave him flattering attention.

"Work at the Town Hall, do you? Yes? What's on your mind?"

"Well, we'd been having letters from a chap called Wideman. He had a bee in his bonnet about the council taking down that tree outside his house. It's my job to go through the letters and sort them into groups for the different departments. Well, this chap's fourth letter arrived by the usual eight-thirty post. It was in my box when I got there. My time is nine."

"Yes?"

"Well, this letter said that now a fellow had hanged himself on it, would the Council take the tree down, and the letter got to us on the morning the chap was found dead."

"I don't get it. Yes, by heck, of course I do. The last post in this neighbourhood goes out at nine-fifteen at night, and Dost didn't die until about one o'clock in the morning. It looks as though our Mr. Wideman has some awkward explaining to do. But are you quite certain of the day?"

"Yes, sir."

"We'd have to have the envelope to prove this, you know, my boy, because of the post-mark, and I guess that envelope was thrown away weeks ago."

"I can find the envelope, sir."

"Where?"

"In my salvage sack at the office."

"After all this time?"

"Oh, yes, I don't send the sack away until it's full, and it takes a whole lot of envelopes to fill a sack, sir, even with all the rubbish people write to the Town Hall."

Sammy

Thanks for cautioning me, Chief Inspector, but there isn't any need. Of course, I'll tell you what happened. I'll tell you just as I told the captain, Captain Coppensen, of the liner *Mountain Isla*.

Oh! Yes, sir, I know she's only a three thousand ton–er, but she's a liner, all the same, because she sticks to a line, she'd don't tramp, if you get me.

Pete Higgins and me, we was cook and cook's mate. Always signed on together, and got on a fair treat. Nothing don't seem the same without old Pete. Well, what happened was this, and it was much as usual excepting the way things ended.

The ship left Liverpool with a cargo of dried fish and some steel girders, and it was a dead easy passage to Funchal where we unloaded some of the fish and took aboard some wicker chairs and a good few cases of old Madeira wine.

After Funchal it wasn't quite so good, but nothing much to grumble about — it's sometimes a bit choppy on the run from Funchal to Tenerife. We didn't have no grouse, but some of the passengers felt it a bit, so I heard.

Yes sir, we carried passengers. Only just sufficient to sit at the captain's table — three or four, usually, and always men or married people on account we don't carry a stewardess.

Well, after we left Funchal, Pete says to me to look out for Sammy. Sammy was our shark. We used to look out for him every voyage. We made quite a pet of him, because he used to follow the ship to get the food we threw out to him. A lot of food gets wasted on board ship, you'd be surprised.

x

Anyway, all that there was Sammy had. He would turn belly up and open his mouth and give us a kind of a wink and a grin. Then in would go the meat and bread and stuff, and then Sammy would roll over and disappear till we had something else to throw to him.

He wasn't what you'd call a big feller — not for a shark. I've seen 'em three times as big in the Pacific — and he was kind of playful. We thought a lot of Sammy, Pete and me did, and we used to reckon he sort of knew us.

We had a hard job, sometimes, to keep him to ourselves and stop the deck-hands feeding him, but we was better off than them because all they'd got was the bits left off of their plates, whereas from us Sammy could get a mutton leg with plenty of meat left on it, and lots of stale soft-tack and things like that. We never used shin of beef for nothing in the cooking line, not while Sammy was around to take his perks.

Well, we spotted him just after six bells in the afternoon watch. All the dinners was done with, and we was taking it easy laying in the sun out on the main deck forrard. I spots him first and points him out to Pete.

"There's Sammy," I says. "Let's go give him the scrapings."

So we done that, and he sheered off when we'd give him what we'd been saving up for him. He was never no nuisance. When we told him that was the last he always believed us.

Well, he was back again, as usual next morning, for his fat bacon and fried bread — he dearly loved his breakfast, did Sammy! and he followed us into port, like he always had.

We tied up to the Mole at Santa Cruz, but the water's deep and if you was to look over the side away from the Mole you might think you was still out at sea.

It's a nice spot. You'd think, near the Mole like that, the water would be too dirty for swimming in, but it isn't, and u hands used to drop a rope ladder overside and climb down into the water.

At least, that's what we done before Sammy came along. But naturally he put paid to them sort of larks, so we used to take one of the life-boats when we got shore leave, and pull around to the beach and swim there.

The beach is nice at Tenerife, sir, but owing to the duty rota, the two of us, Pete and me, we didn't get shore leave that particular afternoon. I mean the afternoon when Pete died. We wasn't the only ones left aboard, but we was on deck, and the others, they was having a kip down, excepting Mr. Wilks. He was down below, checking stores.

×

No, Pete and me did not chew the fat together and fight on deck that afternoon, and neither did I ever say, the day before, to Pete, that if he was all that fond of Sammy he could go and make his better acquaintance.

That there Nobby Clark what told you that, he's had it in for me ever since I uppercut him into the canal for speaking insulting about my young lady, and if he says me and Pete was chewing the fat about Sammy or anything else, he's a liar, which he is, anyway. And we certainly didn't fight.

No, I would not call myself a quarrelsome man. I could tell you what that there Nobby Clark called my young lady, if you like, and then you could see the provocation I had.

Get on with the story? All right. But I'm warning you it ain't a story, it's the sober solid truth, which is more than Nobby ever told in his life. And if he ever says we had a fight on deck, and I knifed Pete and chucked him overboard, well, you ought to know what to think, as I do, too.

There wasn't no knifing in it. No, what happens is this. Being as it was a nice afternoon, I says ain't it a pity Sammy being there and us not able to go into the water with him, so Pete bets me I won't go overside for a swim.

"You needn't mind Sammy," he says, "because he's late for his dinner already, and he'll be hanging about round the galley porthole where I can hold him easy enough for the two or three minutes as you'll be in the water and you can watch us from there as well, to see fair play."

Look here, if I do it, will you follow suit? I says. We gets to daring each other and raising the bets till at last I agrees, though I didn't much fancy the caper.

×

There's the rope ladder hanging overside, and I goes down first into the galley with Pete to make sure as Sammy really is outside the porthole — well, it's more of a half-door, really, but it can be all battened up in rough weather. Sammy's there all right, and giving us a bit of an old-fashioned look for keeping him waiting so long.

Well, I've got my bathing trunks on — we're in port, see? — and I nips up on deck and I'm soon in the briny, splashing hard just to make sure Sammy don't have a sniff. Though, of course, from where I am, aft, I can see the galley port all right, and make sure Pete's keeping him busy.

Well, then I climbs up on deck again — ever tried climbing a rope ladder on to a ship's deck, Inspector? You ought to have a go sometime — it ain't all that easy — and Sammy and Pete is still sparring about down below, and plenty of grub still left for me to keep Sammy busy while Pete has his swim.

"You'll be sure to keep track of him, won't you?" says poor old Pete. "Because he ain't as hungry as he was while you was in the water."

×

He bunks off full pelt, and I rubs meself with me towel with one hand, and feeds Sammy with the other. It's rare fun feeding a shark. There's a kind of a swirl in the water, and then there's his big white waistcoat what he opens his mouth out of, and there he is, upside down like a bloke doing flying stunts in a crate.

All of a sudden, when I heaves him a chunk of fat bacon, one of his favourite tit-bits, I don't see no tail, nor I don't see no belly. I has wind-up proper at that so I lobs over another chunk of the bacon and hares up on deck to warn Pete as Sammy has finished his dinner.

There was Pete all right, splashing away to make sure Sammy kept his distance, and I leans over and I hollers at him fit to burst me bellows, but he never hears me.

So I climb over the side and down the rope ladder to get on a line with him, see, but I'm too late, see? Just as I gets within four feet of the water-line I sees him go under, and then I sees Sammy lashing and swirling with Pete's legs between his jaws.

×

What do you mean — tell you another one? I'm telling you what I told the skipper, no more and no less. Explain the — what was the word? — discrepancies in my story? Oh, where it don't fit together?

But it do fit, inspector! What do you take me for? It all happened just like I told you, and Nobby Clark can talk his something head off.

It's his word against mine, and I'm entitled to the benefit of the doubt. You won't get no more out of me than what I've told you already. Me and Pete never chewed the fat together, and that's that; and nor did we fight, neither; and nor did I knife him. Why should I?

How do I explain the shark going away before he ate the bacon? I don't have to explain it. I just something well don't know.

How do I explain Sammy couldn't have took Pete's leg between his jaws? But he did, that's all I'm telling you.

How do I explain Sammy wasn't a man-eating shark, but only a basker? How do you expect *me* to know the difference? How do I explain why, if Sammy didn't want the fat bacon he *did* want Pete? I can't read a shark's thoughts, can I?

How do I explain — well, yes, the rope ladder and the galley part *was* on the same side of the ship. I said so, didn't I?

How do I explain that if I could see Pete feeding Sammy, why couldn't Pete see me? Why did I run up on deck when he might have heard me if I'd stopped down below?

How do I explain — ? Why don't I come clean? Tell you what really happened? Blimey, I *have* told you what really happened.

Oh, they've found the body, have they? A knife-wound in the back? Search me, it don't make sense. My knife? Let you take my finger-prints? Well, they'd be on my knife, naturally. No, you can't prove nothing, Inspector, except, barring Sammy, Pete was the best friend I got.

Oh, all right, then. I did knife him. And I did tumble him overboard. And for why? It wasn't Nobby Clark, it was Pete as insulted my young lady.

Peach Jam

The sudden death of Mr. Phillips came as a shock. But this news was as nothing compared with the effect of the further information that he had been poisoned with cyanide of potassium, known in its distilled and more deadly form as prussic acid.

Mr. Phillips had been living alone, his wife on holiday, at the time of his death, and the first intimation that something was wrong had been the accumulation of milk-bottles on his doorstep. The milkman informed the police, the police broke in, and the body was discovered in the dining-room.

Macabre and yet curiously touching was the state of the room, for Mr. Phillips had been having his tea. An overturned cup stained the cloth and dripped on to the carpet, a book, *The Adventures of Huckleberry Finn*, was propped against the sugar bowl, and a half-eaten piece of bread spread with peach jam had dropped jam-side downwards, on the hearth-rug.

The body, after the police surgeon examined it, had been taken to a mortuary. Horrid, but vital evidence of the contents of teapot, sugar bowl and milk jug had been sent for analysis, together with the piece of bread-and-jam and the contents of the half-consumed jar.

The evidence of the stomach was conclusive. Part of the contents consisted of a chewed-up mass of peach kernels. But the curious thing was that no kernels could be discovered in the jam.

Detective-inspector Pritchard was assigned to the case, for the coroner's jury brought in a verdict of Murder by Person or Persons Unknown, in spite of a strong hint from their presiding genius that suicide would be an equally sound hypothesis.

×

Mrs. Phillips, who had been staying with her mother, returned home as soon as the dreadful news reached her. She identified the body as that of her husband, and was questioned by the police. She took them to her store-cupboard and showed them a dozen pots of home-made peach jam, none of which contained kernels.

Questioned on this point, she said she had never realised that her husband liked the kernels and so had never troubled to put them in.

The police impounded the jam and sent all twelve pots for analysis, but these received a clean bill from the laboratory.

Reluctantly, Detective-inspector Pritchard abandoned suspicions of Mrs. Phillips and transferred his attention to the dead man's private life.

This was found to be interesting rather than virtuous. There was no doubt that Mr. Phillips was one of those who, in the words of the old ballad, had had a sweetheart in Gairloch Wells, or, in his particular case, about two miles from his home. But this young lady, a certain Miss Smith who had been Mr. Phillips's private secretary at one time, never made jam of any kind, but bought it, a pound pot at a time, whenever Mr. Phillips (about whose patronage she was perfectly frank) could sneak away from his wife and come to stay the weekend with her.

"He loved jam," she said. "The only row we ever had was when he told me how delicious his wife's home-made jam was, and how much he missed it when he stayed with me."

×

The detective-inspector, who was nothing if not thorough, went to the shops which she patronised and inspected all the jars of jam, but no peach jam was to be seen. Apricot, yes, but peach, no. There was no call for it, announced the shop assistant.

This led nowhere, but it began to look as if there might be a *prima facie* case against Miss Smith since, when Mr. Phillips's will was proved, it transpired that though more than half his property was assigned to his wife, he had left a comfortable little nest-egg to secure to Miss Smith the continued enjoyment of the flat and the carefree life of a lady of leisure.

Mrs. Phillips, on the other hand, brought herself back into unwelcome limelight by making the statement that she had known of Miss Smith's existence for some time and had had no objection to her influence over the husband.

"Far from it," were her words. "He was a hard-working man and he deserved a little relaxation. I've always been broad-minded. I hope."

It was this provocative statement which made Detective-inspector Pritchard even more suspicious of her than he had been at the beginning.

"It's incredible, or nearly so," he said to Sergeant Staples. "No wife will ever admit that the other woman can give her husband something she herself can't. It's unnatural, and I don't like unnatural things. There's always something phoney about them. I smell a rat, Staples. Let's track it to its hole."

"Just so, sir," said the sergeant, who was a bachelor and who intended, women being willing, to remain so. He spoke respectfully. He had met Mrs. Phillips, and, had he been passing private judgment, would have admitted that he did not like her.

"That woman has something up her sleeve," went on Pritchard, "and that something is murder."

He was notably painstaking officer even in a service where the taking of pains results very often in success. He went to work at first on the simple theory that Mrs. Phillips had contrived to poison the peach kernels without poisoning the jam they were in, but apart from the fact that this seemed an impossible feat in itself, nobody could have foreseen that her husband would take out every kernel at one and the same time and so provide himself with a fatal dose of the poison. For, according to the analyst's account, it was unlikely that one or two of the kernels would have done any harm. Allowing for the medicinal effects of minute quantities of the drug, they might even have done good.

x

Pritchard combed through the poisons books in the local chemists' shops but found no mention of the sale of cyanide of potassium, still less of a sale of prussic acid. It was a curious and disheartening case, but at last the sergeant obtained a pointer which led to the solution of the mystery.

"I've been mixing round again, sir, where the young lady, Miss Smith lives. Did you know that before she took up with Mr. Phillips and the flat she was employed by a firm of electro-plate people.

"I recollected that in electro-plating they use cyanide of potassium, which, when distilled, provides prussic acid, the very poison we're after. So it just struck me to wonder whether Phillips himself or one of the two ladies had ever been in the electro-plate line or else very interested in photography.

"Well, it turns out that before she went into Mr. Phillips' office she'd had this other job. She only stopped in it six months before she came under Mr. Phillips's protection (as I believe they call it, sir), but six months is quite long enough to find out that the firm uses quite considerable quantities of cyanide of potassium, so I thought I'd just pass on the hint, sir."

Pritchard interviewed Miss Smith. She admitted at once that she had indeed worked in the office of the firm specialising in electro-plate but she denied all knowledge of their processes and claimed that the office staff had nothing to do with the practical side of the business. She did not know until Pritchard told her, that there was any connection between prussic acid (of which she had heard, although vaguely) and cyanide of potassium, of which she claimed she had no knowledge at all.

×

Pritchard was puzzled and disappointed. What had seemed a promising clue had come to nothing, for a visit he paid to the firm in question had resulted in the unhelpful information that while there was no particular reason why the office staff should *not* have known something of the firm's processes, on the other hand there was equally no reason why they should. They confirmed that Miss Smith had only been with them for six months.

Baffled and disappointed, Pritchard sat down to think over the problem again. He felt inclined to throw in his hand and tell his superiors that the mystery was insoluble. Then something struck him like lightning, a flash of revelation which made him curse himself for a dim-witted fool.

"Staples," he said, "what was Phillips doing, living alone in his house when, with his wife away, he had Miss Smith and the flat to go to?"

The sergeant's jaw dropped comically, but he leapt to the right conclusion.

"You mean he *wasn't* alone when he died, sir? You mean, instead of him going to Miss Smith, she was staying at his place with him for a bit of a change?"

"If she wasn't I'll burn my uniform and join the nudists, Staples. Now you get on to the neighbours and I'll go and sort out that block of flats where she lives."

He had no success at the flats, which were inhabited by business or professional people who had almost nothing to do with each other. None of them had noticed or would have bothered whether Miss Smith was occupying her flat or not.

There was only one clue. The milkman had not called at her flat for 10 days. Challenged, he showed his order book. He had been told not to call.

×

The sergeant was unlucky, too.

"It wouldn't do to mention *everything* one suspects," said the elderly woman who lived in the detached house next door to Phillips's home, "and I could not possibly undertake to say who visited Mr. Phillips and who did not. I never saw anyone there, and that I *do* know. I should never *dream* of spying on my neighbours."

Staples inwardly cursed her, but had to report failure. The cancellation of the milk had decided Pritchard, however. He took the sergeant with him, went to Miss Smith, cautioned her, and said:

"I have reason to believe that you were present when Mr. Phillips was poisoned. I have reason to suspect that you took with you a number of peach kernels poisoned with prussic acid in its form (as used in the electro-plate industry) of cyanide of potassium. I suggest that you administered the poisoned kernels to Mr. Phillips, thereby causing his death and I warn you that anything you say will be taken down and may be used in evidence."

×

Miss Smith broke down.

"He was always twitting me about his wife's jam," she said. "If you call that loving me, I don't. All right, I took a pas'n-pot with me. The kernels were in it and I mixed in some of his wife's jam. I fed it him with a spoon, jollying him all the time. I don't think I meant to kill him. I wanted to teach him a lesson."

"But there's the matter of the legacy," said Pritchard later. "That was her real motive. The fool must have told her about it."

Staples shook his head. He reflected that his decision to have nothing to do with women was a sound one.

The Plumb-Line

The queerest case I ever struck (said the ex-detective-inspector) was that of Hawk and Partridge. Hawk lived on the top floor of Partridge's small suburban house and Partridge's was perfectly safe from him until two things happened to put Partridge's life in danger.

The first was that Partridge, a widower, married again. She was a young and pretty woman with whom Hawk, through no fault of his own, fell violently in love. She was flighty and of no particular strength of character.

She did not love Hawk — in fact there is no evidence that she loved anybody except herself — but he soon came to the conclusion that she liked him better than she liked her dull and rather elderly husband.

But, infatuated with her although Hawk was, Partridge might still have had nothing to fear had not a second event occurred. Partridge won a large sum of money on the Pools.

Hawk, who (we found out later) had been getting into debt, chewed over his own troubles and other people's luck, brooded a bit and then decided to play Fate's hand by killing Partridge and, after a respectable interval and provided he wasn't caught, marry the widow and, of course, the money. The only difficulty was to think up a safe way of doing the job.

The thing which seems to have given him the idea which he worked up into a plan was the fact that Partridge had a bald head. This fascinated Hawk. If only he could drop something pretty heavy on it and make the thing look like an accident the deed would be done and he would have nothing to fear.

The trouble was that this could only be tried once. In other words, he mustn't fail. Well he overdid the thing. He felt he must have practise, and it wasn't the sort of thing to practise in secret, so he let it be understood that he had invented a new religion.

He gave up going to the cinema; he gave up drinking — of which he was very fond — he even gave up going to football matches. Instead of all this he played with a plumb-line. It was just a piece of whipcord with a smallish weight on the end. His idea was to increase the weight until he was using something heavy enough to kill Partridge.

×

He seems to have done the thing thoroughly. He fastened the weight with a cradle of yellow silk and explained (to anyone who asked) that the colour stood for happiness and that when he had achieved happiness he would alter the colour and try for concentration, the power of contemplation.

Hawk invented a sort of fishing-rod with a pulley so that instead of having to sit on the balcony railings over the french doors he could recline in a chair and drop the plumb-line and wind it in again. Partridge, who was childlike in a way, decided to have a plumb-line for himself, and they used to practise dropping the weights on to smaller and smaller objects, taking turns to go below to report on one another's progress.

×

There seems to be some maniac law that every new religion, however crazy or phony, is bound to attract disciples. Partridge was only the first. Soon there were six other serious thinkers among the neighbours, all methodically dropping the weight and winding it in.

This suited Hawk completely.

At last he decided that the time was ripe to put his plan into action. The early temptation to drop the heavy weight he was now using on to Partridge's bald head as the man came out through the french doors below the balcony he had abandoned as being impracticable. Both Partridge and his wife had given up using the french doors for fear of accidents.

Hawk had made up his mind that a theatre was the best place in which to carry out his plan. Whilst the Partridges were on holiday he made a round of the smaller London theatres until he found a suitable one for his purpose. It had a centre gangway to the stalls whose entrance was from the back of the pit. The dress circle was in two segments and also had a central gangway. It might all have been constructed to Hawk's special design.

But before he could make a foolproof plan of campaign a curious coincidence happened. After his return from holiday Partridge presented him with a couple of tickets for the very theatre which he himself had chosen as the place for the murder.

"The little woman is crazy to see this show," said Partridge, "and so I bought a couple of seats. But now I've been told I'm to go to Blackpool.

"I wonder, old man, if you'd oblige me? She's been looking forward to it so much, and she doesn't get much fun nowadays."

Hawk was nearly dizzy with delight. He took the tickets and promised to accompany Mrs. Partridge to the show. He was quite prepared to abandon his plumb-line just for one evening, he said.

×

His experiments with heavier and heavier weights, while undoubtedly of great spiritual value, had begun to produce some rather alarming symptoms. His doctor had tested him and had told him that he had overstrained his heart.

Hawk and Mrs. Partridge did not get to the theatre very early, and there was the usual last minute confusion of people in the foyer and gangways all showing tickets and buying programmes.

Suddenly, to everybody's consternation, Hawk gave a groan and fell heavily.

A doctor in the audience came immediately, but there was nothing to be done for Hawk. He was stone dead. Heart-failure.

×

The ex-inspector sat back and sipped his drink. His audience looked puzzled.

"But I don't see why you call it your most curious case," said one. "I can't see it was any case at all."

"Well, Partridge was in the theatre, you see. He hadn't gone to Blackpool. That was only a blind. Some men in the circle had been prompt to grab him as soon as Hawk fell, because they had seen him drop something on to Hawk's head.

"So we were called in to investigate. Hawk showed no sign of injury, however, and the medical evidence was clear. Death from heart failure, possibly caused by shock.

Partridge showed us what he'd used. It was simply a tennis ball on the end of a strong elastic. It couldn't have killed anybody.

"He admitted that he had entertained suspicions of his wife and Hawk, and had decided to watch them while they thought he was away on business. He'd gone to the theatre ahead of them.

"When he saw them, however, he felt ashamed of his suspicions, and, deciding to attract their attention and invite them to a drink in the interval, and enjoy their surprise when they found he hadn't gone to Blackpool after all, he had remembered the tennis ball in his pocket. He thought he would drop it on to Hawk's bare head for a joke."

"But there was nothing in that to base a charge on, was there?" inquired another of his hearers. The ex-inspector shook his head. "Not a thing," he replied cheerfully.

"The end of the story came later, after the Partridges had emigrated on the strength of the pools money Partridge had won. He'd only left England a year when he, too, died — of heart failure due to overstrain. There aren't any plumb-line addicts now.

"After his death Mrs. Partridge came clean and wrote to us. As she wasn't legally any kind of accessory we had nothing on her, you see.

"She told us that she got terribly frightened because she had an inkling, from hints he'd let fall, that Hawk intended mischief on her husband. She told Partridge of the balcony meetings, but swore that she herself intended no harm. Partridge appears to have forgiven her, but he told her he should get back on Hawk.

"Well, so he did, of course. And what he did, in my opinion, was to murder him. And that's why I call it my queerest case."

Haunted House

Seen through the window the landscape was wintry and bare. "Better in spring," said John Graham. He turned away from the window and looked at the fire of logs. "But it's cosy enough in here. How do you like it, Morag?"

"I like it very well," his wife replied, "but you did not tell me it was haunted."

"Haunted? Who said so?"

"It was the agent. He said it was nothing to hurt."

"Oh that!" Her husband laughed it off. "It was just his nonsense. You've been seeing too much of him, Morag. He did say something to me. Just sounds, he said, as one gets in any old house."

"Yes, John, but what about the footprints?"

John Graham frowned.

"If you don't think you'll be happy here — " he began. But she laughed and called him her darling and said that she liked the house well.

×

One day Morag broached the subject of the haunting to the agent when he came for the rent.

He denied the rumours hotly, but admitted that the house had a bad name in the neighbourhood.

"But maybe folk have been frightened," she suggested.

"Well, I don't know about that," he answered, accepting the hint. "What are a few odd noises? There's no danger, I can assure you." He got up to go, but she detained him.

"Francis, I know you won't deceive me. Have you heard anything yourself?"

He hesitated; then he answered.

"Twice, but it didn't amount to much. Just noises and something that sounded like footsteps, you know."

"What about the footprints splashed with blood?"

"I never heard of any such thing, nor saw it, either. It's old wives' tales you've been hearing."

Time passed, spring drew near and the agent became a less frequent visitor. Nothing ghostly was seen or heard.

Then rumour began again. The village at that time of the year had little to gossip about, so it continued to remark upon the number of times the agent still visited the house, and to speculate, not too kindly, upon the reason.

The gossip was kept from Morag this time, but between her and her husband something hovered in the air, something intangible, invisible and silent.

She proposed that they should give a little party to the half-dozen friends they had made. He agreed — heavily, she thought.

But the party was not a success.

When the first guests left, it was snowing. Between the black of the night and the glow from the house the large flakes swirled and melted, spinning like stars or softly falling like leaves. Huddling their coats against the snowfall, the departing guests stole away, themselves no more than ghosts as the snow settled down on their shoulders.

At last only one guest was left, the agent, Francis. At half-past eleven he, too, declared that he must go. He went for his coat and scarf. Graham went to the front and looked out. The snow was already in drift and was falling faster than before.

Graham withdrew from the door, closed it and put his back against it. When Francis came into the hall he said in belligerent tones:

"You'll never reach home. You'll never get through tonight. You'd better have our room. Morag can sleep in the warm down here on the settee, and I have a camp bed I use when I come in late."

The house, supposed to be haunted, had no near neighbours, so that no one except the three who slept there that night could say when the sounds began. They had retired at just after midnight — both witnesses were agreed upon that. But after that their stories varied, although they were taken over them time and again. One man, the police decided, was lying, and the other was telling the truth.

×

Graham told the sergeant in charge that he had found Morag, his wife, dead on the dining-room floor when he went to call her in the morning. She had been sleeping in the drawing-room on the settee.

He had rushed out for the village doctor, hoping against hope that something could be done. Morag Graham had been stabbed and had been dead for several hours by the time the doctor arrived. Graham had then collapsed, and Francis had run for the police.

Later, when the police had seen and photographed the body and the room in which it had been found, and had taken finger-prints and looked for clues, Graham told his full story.

He said that the three of them — himself, Morag and Francis, had separated at just after midnight, and that Morag had had a cup of cocoa and the two men had each drunk a nightcap of whisky and water. As it had proved impossible for Francis to get home that night, he had been offered a bed.

x

Graham knew no more until he had gone to wake his wife and suggest that it was time for a cup of tea and breakfast. He had found her stabbed in the back, her progress from the drawing-room being marked by her own blood-stained footprints.

"You think, then," said the inspector, "that your wife was attacked in the drawing-room, staggered into the dining-room and there collapsed and died?"

Graham did think so, and appeared to be deeply affected.

The police then asked Francis for a statement. He gave substantially the same account as Graham had done, except for one particular. He had been awakened, he alleged, at about four in the morning by sounds which he could not interpret.

Asked to describe the sounds, he said that they resembled scuffling and moaning. He had lighted his bedside candle and had sat up to listen. He had also looked at his watch.

"How long did the sounds continue?" he was asked.

"About three or four minutes, but it might have been longer."

"Why didn't you go and investigate?"

"I knew the house was said to be haunted, so I didn't bother."

"Didn't it occur to you that one of the Grahams might have been taken ill?"

"No, it never occurred to me, and if it had, I should have thought it no business of mine as there would have been the other one there."

"What happened after that?"

"Nothing, so far as I know. I just lay down and went to sleep again. We'd had rather a lot to drink during the evening so I may still have been a bit fuddled."

"I see. Now what about these sleeping arrangements. Who made them?"

"It was Graham himself."

"Not Mrs. Graham?"

"Well, they may have talked it over in the kitchen. I wouldn't know about that. It was certainly Graham who mentioned them to me."

"Didn't they seem to you rather peculiar?"

"Yes, but it wasn't any business of mine."

Graham was recalled.

"Who decided that Francis should occupy the double bed?"

"My wife and I agreed about it. Francis was a wee bit drunk and we thought maybe he would tumble out of the camp bed or off the settee. We didn't want that. It would have frightened my wife."

"Better be frightened than dead," thought the officer grimly, but naturally did not give voice to this opinion. There seemed no other evidence available.

×

The medical evidence agreed well enough with the time given by Francis, and the snow had ceased at just after two in the morning, so that it was clear that no stranger had approached the house.

All the footprints in the snow could be identified as being those of the two men and the police. It was a curious and baffling case. Even the weapon did not help.

Mrs. Graham had been stabbed with a Zulu assegai which had been hanging on the drawing-room wall. It had been wiped clear of finger-prints and hung up again, and it was sufficiently long for the murderer to have avoided getting blood on his clothing, although both men's garments had been meticulously examined.

"Well, there it is," said the inspector to the Chief Constable.

"One of them did it, sir, and of course there's no trouble about the motive. It's a sex crime all right. There appears to have been a rare lot of gossip about it in the village — the affair between Mrs. Graham and Francis, I mean.

"Personally, I'd put my money on Graham. He seems to have had a lot to put up with, if rumour can be believed. But there's no actual evidence one way or the other so far as I can see. You can't hang a man on probability only. The only thing I can suggest is to arrest them both, charge them jointly, and let the magistrates sort it out."

×

"You know, it's that arrangement about the sleeping that puzzles me," said the Chief Constable. "I mean, is it reasonable to hand over the only comfortable bed in the house to a man guest and expect your wife to sleep on the settee?"

"It may have been the wife's arrangement, you know, sir."

"Yes, there's that, of course. I wonder why she made for the dining-room when she was attacked? And why there was no blood on the settee?"

"I don't know, sir."

"I wonder whether we ought to attach any importance to the fact that none of the three could have known beforehand that Francis was going to stay the night?"

"I don't really think so, sir. One of them suddenly saw an opportunity and seized it. I should say. And, of course, they were both pretty drunk, apparently, and men will do things under the influence which normally they wouldn't think of doing, however much they might secretly want to."

"That's true enough, but it doesn't help us if they were both drunk. It means it's as long as it's broad. Let's go over it again. There might be something we've overlooked. Yes! By Jove! I think we've got him! Have him in again."

×

Graham looked haggard but defiant.

"Can't you leave me alone?" he asked. "I've told you over and over again that I don't know anything more."

"I'm going to tell you, not ask you, this time," said the Chief Constable. "I'll tell you exactly what happened. You can correct me if I go wrong.

"I suggest that you deliberately arranged the sleeping so that you could confirm your suspicions of your wife and Francis. You thought she would take the risk of going to him in that double bed. Instead of going to the camp bed you sneaked into the kitchen from where you could keep track of the proceedings.

"Your suspicions proved to be well-founded. As soon as your wife rose from the settee you rushed in and snatched down the assegai. She fled from you — not up the stairs (for she realised that that would not save her) but into the dining-room where she hoped to be able to slam the door on you. You were a little too quick for her.

"I'm sorry for you, Graham, but the officer must make his arrest. She *must* have got up off that settee, for there was no blood on it."

×

This reasoning broke Graham down.

"There's one thing, sir," said the inspector soberly. "Whether that house was haunted before this happened I wouldn't really care to say, but I reckon it's haunted now."

The Falling Petals

"The act was a cinch," said Detective-inspector Bentam thoughtfully. His sergeant looked hopeful. The inspector sighed. "And that's where we begin and end," he concluded.

"We could recapitulate, sir." his subordinate suggested.

"All right. You do it."

"It was a good act," said the sergeant. "Pretty, skilful and daring. Five people took part. There were Dad, Mum, the Wonder Boy, Borzoi and Baby. They had all been born to the job except the Wonder Boy, who had become too old for the same sort of work on the pictures, and so had joined the troupe four years before Dad's death. All right, sir?"

"Yes. Go on. It doesn't get us any further so far."

"No, sir. Dad and Mum had one child called Baw. She is a half-wit, having fallen on her head as a baby. She took no part in the show, but attended all the rehearsals, and, according to her mother, was interested in all that the troupe did.

"The act was called The Falling Petals, and fall, in a sense, was all that the troupe had to do. But there was usually a row going on between Dad and Borzoi as to which of them should fall last.

"It appears that the act consisted of the artistes swinging themselves down on a series of silk loops. It was easy enough for the first one because the loops were still. All that was needed here was a certain amount of gymnastic ability. All correct so far, sir?"

"Couldn't be better. Go on."

"As the descents went on they became progressively more difficult. The last one down had a particularly sticky task, because by the lime four others had done the stunt the silk loops were swinging so much that the very nicest judgment was required to pull off the last lap. The loops were unweighted and seemed to swing aimlessly. All the same, Borzoi was convinced that he could manage Dad's trick, and should be allowed to try."

"All correct. Then what?"

"In the end, Borzoi held up Dad by threatening to join another troupe if he couldn't have his own way. Dad stalled — said he would think it over — and things remained as they were.

"Then suddenly Dad copped it. He fell and broke his neck. Reason? One of the silken loops had been cut almost through. It had borne Baby, Mum, the Wonder Boy, and Borzoi, in that order, but it broke under Dad. Interesting, sir, don't you think?"

"Very. Go on."

"The trouble, as I see it, sir, is whether the right person fell. It seems to me that you'd need the deuce of a lot of knowledge and experience to cut a loop on which five people were going to swing to be sure you'd get the right one to break his neck."

"If so, that might let Borzoi out. He's been the likeliest suspect so far."

"Yes, sir. The more you think of it, the less likely it seems that it was Borzoi who did the deed. He was number four out of five, and I should say that he risked his own neck almost equally with Dad's if he'd been the one to cut the loop.

"I don't believe it was Borzoi, sir. I believe the drop was intended for Borzoi, not for Dad. Why don't we try that for a working hypothesis?"

"Go ahead, Sergeant."

"You see, supposing the drop was really intended for Borzoi, we get a new set of suspects one of whom could even have been Dad himself."

"No, you can't tell me that one, my lad. Borzoi came down safely, remember. You don't tell me that if the plan had misfired, and Dad had made that plan, he would have been fool enough to break his own neck?"

"There are two answers to that, sir. The first is that, as the cut loop had borne Borzoi, Dad may have concluded that it would also bear him. Borzoi is heavier than Dad.

"Secondly supposing that Dad had stalled and made the excuse that the loop wasn't safe, what would everybody have thought? Why, that he had made the attempt on Borzoi's life and was practically confessing to it.

"And Dad had a pretty good motive, mind you, for killing the boy. Either he had to give way to him and let him take the place of honour in the troupe or else he had to lose him to a rival concern. Now could I give you the dossiers again, sir?"

"Do."

"Well sir, the dossiers go like this: First there's Mum, legally married to Dad and, so far as we know, quite fond of him. Somehow I can't see Mum murdering Dad, sir."

"Agreed. Go on."

"Then there's Wonder Boy. He might have been affected by jealousy, but he's got his head screwed on all right, and he must have guessed that when Dad was dead there wasn't much chance for him to remain in the troupe."

"Why do you say that? You've nothing to go on, have you?"

"Not exactly, sir, but Wonder Boy isn't much good nowadays. He's getting past it, and he drinks. Once he's finished with the troupe he's finished altogether, I fancy. I don't believe he'd have killed Dad. It was tantamount to killing the goose with the golden eggs. So the two left are Borzoi and Baby."

"And the half-wit Baw, don't forget. Personally, I rather incline to Baw. It was a nit-wit proposition to iron out Dad."

"Quite so, sir. But apart from poor Baw we've still got Borzoi and Baby, and those two — neither is any relation of Mum or Dad — are in love and want to get married. With Dad out of the way and Borzoi boss of the troupe they'd have a good deal more money to get married on. Mum told me she was already pretty sure that Borzoi means to chisel her out of part of her share of the takings. Not altogether a nice type, that lad."

"Motive, eh? Then there's another pair who might have one. What about, a put-up job between Mum and Wonder Boy?"

"Collusion so that the two of them could get married, you mean, sir? Could be, of course. Would it be any good asking the four of them to do their act for us and see where the reactions fitted in?"

"I can't see how it would help. You might easily get an innocent person proving far more nervous than the murderer. Besides, they would almost certainly refuse to cooperate, and I don't see how we could compel them.

"No. I'm afraid we shall get no more evidence. Look here, my boy, one of them did it. Surely it isn't beyond us to work out which one?"

"I have worked it out, sir. You see, there's one thing to which we haven't given quite enough attention, and that is to find out which of them had the opportunity to cut the loop. It wasn't done during the performance because that would be impossible. Ergo. It was done before the act started."

"Granted. If we could show who could have had access to the loops before the show we'd be able to point to the murderer.

"But you know what the trouble has been all the time about that. Everybody — and that includes the stage-manager, a man who's got no other connection with these people — everybody swears that nobody except Dad ever had the loops in his possession. They were kept under lock and key and were personally tested by Dad before they were put up, and they weren't put up until the change of act, and then always under Dad's own supervision."

"Yes, sir, I know. But what I'm pointing out is both clear and logical."

"Oh, nonsense, my boy! Why, it was suicidal for Dad to swing himself down if he knew the rope was cut!"

"Exactly, sir. It was suicidal. I've come to the conclusion that this wasn't murder. It was a very spectacular suicide. After all, why should Dad have broken his neck? He was a very skilful gymnast, and these people learn how to fall. He'd certainly have contrived to land on his feet."

"You can break your neck that way, too."

"Very well, sir. It's not essential to my argument, but the next point is, of all those people, Dad was the only person who had access to the loops and he would have known much better than any of the others the breaking strain of tire silk.

"Nobody else would have been absolutely certain that the right person was going to be killed. Dad was sick of life. Either he'd got to give in to Borzoi or lose him, and, with him, Baby as well, for once they were married, Baby would have followed her husband as soon as she possibly could.

"With those two gone, the act was as good as done for. He couldn't see any way out. He couldn't give in and take second place to Borzoi. These acrobats are as touchy as foreign prima donnas over anything that touches the dignity of their art.

"Dad had designed the act, too — it was in every way his creation — and he'd named it The Falling Petals. Well, the last petal fell — just literally that. There's the logic of the case, sir, don't you think?"

The Price of Lead

Tom Wrenn was a queer sort. Nobody could quite make him out until the war came and they dropped a stick of bombs on our village. Then Tom he come to the fore and behaved like a wonder.

Rector took charge, and Squire, but Tom, I reckon he done the real organising, particularly digging for the buried. So good he dug, and made all of us chaps dig, that we had hospital cases but no casualties.

After that he got quite a position in the village and was made cricket umpire and football ref. and used to help Ted Innis, publican, when he run the beer tent at village fêtes.

Well, time passed, and the war was over, and then there was news of this here church roof caper after lead. Us held a vestry meeting about it, and Rector he wondered whether us best insure against the thieves.

"They be working all over the country," he says, "and if us lose lead off church roof, who be going to pay to put it back?"

×

Well, insurance, that do seem to come rather heavy, and maybe it's money paid out for nothing, so some of us chaps we agree to take turns at keeping watch at nights.

"Us done the fire-watching, so us can do the lead-watching," says Frank Mutch; and all of us chaps agreed. Rector were much obliged, and divvied us up into watches. Our village be pretty small compared to some, so there weren't all that big number on us and it were agreed as we should serve once a fortnight, watching in turns, and in twos.

"That be to make sure us don't pinch the lead ourself," says Bill Pent, as liked his joke. So for three or four months us watches. Nothing don't happen, and the missuses they go for to get restless and to say it remind them of when we joined the Home Guard, and attendance, that begin to fall off.

Meanwhile the price of lead, that go on rising, and Rector he get a bit worried. He called another meeting and put it to us chaps straight.

"If you can't do it," he says, "seems to me we'd better insure."

There was humming and hawing of course, and then one or two begins to speak up in favour. But what with the price of lead going up, well, premiums had gone up, too, and there was quite a few long faces when Squire he begins to talk figures.

"Leave it to me," says Tom Wrenn. "For ten bob a week to pay for my grub end extra baccy, I'll do the job all by myself. I ain't afeared of lead thieves, and if so be they do come I'll toll church bell for all I'm worth. I'll sleep in belfry so I'll be handy. Take more than a gang of lead thieves to get the better of me."

×

Well Rector and Squire talked it over and us chaps was thankful to quit the job.

"Tain't likely as anyone will come," says Bill Pent, as one of the first to give up, his missus expecting their first and not caring to be left alone nights, "and fourpence each a week, if Tom Wrenn will do it for that, won't hurt nary one of us." he says.

So that were all settled, and Rector he shook Tom's hand, and Squire he give him five shillings, and I was made treasurer to collect up all the chaps' fourpences and to see that Tom got his fair dough.

Well, that went on for six months and then some of the chaps began to mimble-mamble about the blinking fourpences.

" 'Tis more than us puts into plate on Sundays," grumbles Ted Heath. He says it in front of others in the Fox and Grapes, and there's plenty there to agree with him. "Nothing haven't happened yet," he says, "and seem to me like, as Tom Wrenn be sitting very pretty with his ten bob a week, and that there pneumatic mattress and the sleeping bag as Squire been and give him."

"Ah, nobody ain't going to take the lead from our church," says Sam Giddings, who'd had three beers too many. "We're off the map here," he says, "and nobody ain't coming here, as we all do very well know."

Well, I'm bound to say as that most of the chaps there agreed, and attendance at the church that do begin to fall off.

But there were one chap as never fall off, and that were our key man, Tom Wrenn.

"I be going to do church a bit of good if it's the last thing I do," he says. And sure enough he rung the bell, he took round the plate, he cut grass in church yard — goodness knows what that poor fellow didn't do.

"I be paid for watching Church against they lead thieves," he says, "and, as nothing haven't happened so far, I'll earn my money as best I can."

Well, us all thought as how it would take a good man to talk like that, and as how it were up to us to support him, all the more as he turns teetotal. And then in the papers us hears there be more lead thieves at work.

" 'Tis coming so close," says Rector, "as I do think us shouldn't leave all to Tom Wrenn. Us'll have to insure," he says. So Tom he gets the sack, and the money that went for his pay us put it into the insurance.

x

Well, time passed and us had paid the insurance two years — Tom Wrenn, I'm bound to say, paying his share like the rest — when all seemed to happen at once.

It were the night before the flower show and nobody had thoughts for nought else, so then the plot seemed to be laid and after that it was just who'd a-thought it.

We had the flower show all right, my marigolds coming in second to Alf Twitters's lupins, and Bill Pent's marrow getting in by half an inch in front of Bill Mutch's and then Rector tells us as how the roof have been stripped off the church and the police have decided to call in they chaps from New Scotland Yard.

"But what for?" says Alf Mayhew. "I thought as how we was insured."

"Ah, yes, Alf," says Rector, as always talked grandest when he was most flummoxed, "us are indeed. But them as have done this deed must be brought to book.

"Funny thing is," he says, "that the job were done while all of us was at flower show. Somebody knowed what were up, and whoever done it got away with two hundred pounds' worth of our lead."

"Us insured for two hundred and fifty. Who's grumbling?" asks Tom Wrenn.

"I am," says Rector, speaking sharp, "This is a local job, Tom, and them what knows about it must step forward."

" 'Tis they chaps over to Little Thenken," says All Mayhew. "Them knowed we was having flower show. What about that?"

"We got to be very careful who we accuses," says Rector, and all the rest of us agrees. Ticklish, you see, when one village hate another the way we hate they chaps over to Little Thenken. It were so ticklish, indeed, that Rector he call in a wise woman from Wandles Parva that he knowed on, and this old lady her poke about like a thrush on a lawn questing worms.

"Who wasn't at flower show who ought to a-been?" her asks.

Well, nobody can't answer that, because them that was missing had no interest in flower show whatsoever. There was Billy Shaw the natural, Ted Innis as kept the pub (and dared not close for fear of losing his license), and Tom Wrenn what was in lodgings and hadn't got his own garden.

"Didn't you have beer tent at show, then?" the old lady she asks.

Well, us looked old-fashioned at that. Did seem queer, come to think of it, that Innis as kept the pub and had always been the first to apply for the license hadn't left his wife in charge of pub (what wouldn't do much business, anyhow, while flower show was on) and come himself to serve in the tent.

"Well, there you are, then," old lady her remark. "You'd better have Publican Innis and his son and this here Tom Wrenn arrested for stealing church lead."

"But Wrenn guarded church for months," says Rector, looking real worried. "I'd sooner suspect myself."

"Well, suspect thyself, then," her says tartly. "But, tell me, haven't publican got son as is lorry driver?"

×

Well, her had Rector there proper, of course, and us, too, because young Bert Innis had his lorry, as all of us know. To cut a long story short, they was all brought to book, but us couldn't help having a bit of sympathy with poor old Tom Wrenn.

"Told you I'd do something for church," he says. "Guarded her proper, I did, and guarded her well, so who have more right nor me to try to get a hold of that insurance money?

"I reckoned as how, what with that and the sale of the lead — us was promised £200 — us could pay off the debt on the organ. Still, never mind, Innis and me, us had our fair bit of fun."

"But it was all so dishonest," says Rector, speaking sorrowful. "You must see it that way, men."

"Dishonest?" says old Alf Dyson, speaking as usual, out of turn. "I don't know so much about that. Us have paid up they premiums, haven't us?

"And them there insurance companies, they're nowt but a betting concern. A man's got a right to his bets. Us betted 'em church lead would be stolen, and they betted us it wouldn't. Well, they fools of Londoners have lost. What be dishonest about that?"

"If you don't know at your age, Alf," says Rector, "it's a waste of my time to try and tell you."

But us chaps, us mostly agree with old Alf Dyson, because us haven't got no benefit neither from insurance nor from all that money spent on church-watching, and organ fund be still hanging fire over village.

The Spell

"Interesting," said Mrs. Bradley, studying the exhibit in an engrossed manner which indicated that she meant what she said. "Don't you think so, George?"

Her chauffeur, who, at her invitation, had accompanied her into the small Folk Museum of the town, agreed with more politeness than truth. George lived only for machinery, and of agriculture (except for its mechanical implements) he understood little and cared less.

They were standing in front of a tall, glass-fronted cupboard which displayed corn-babies, those curious, carefully-fashioned little sheaves which bore the likeness of primitive human beings. They were not large — about ten inches, maybe, was the average height — but there was something sinister about them in spite of their appearance of childish innocence.

"A bit of witchcraft, madam, if you ask me," George continued. "Fertility rites, I suppose."

"Your supposition is correct."

"Ah, that it be," said a voice which came from behind them.

"And seeing you knows sommat about it, maybe you'd tell me what I'd best to do."

An elderly man looked rheumily at Mrs. Bradley out of his red-rimmed eyes.

"I can't sleep nor eat," he announced, "and nobody as I knows on in our village be willing to give me a hand. Now you be an eddicated lady, and I'd take it kindly if you was to tell me what I should do for the best."

"Domestic troubles?" Mrs. Bradley inquired.

"Not the way you be meaning; no, not domestic exactly. It's my darter. Her be bewitched, and all along of one of they things there. Work of the devil, um be. Trouble is, her don't know who's at the bottom of it, and me, I don't know neether. Lost her mother when she was seven, and had to look after each other, us have, all these years.

"Her's thirty-five now, and me, I be rising seventy. And now her pines and mopes, and complains all the time about her stomach. Her won't let me call in the doctor. Says he'll tell her nothing be wrong but what watching what her eats won't cure.

" 'Tis the witchcraft doing it, I reckon, and so do she. Ever since she found the corn-baby in her bed her's been like this peeking and pulling and pining."

"Where is the corn-baby now?" Mrs. Bradley inquired.

"Why, in the cupboard, under the stairs. I wanted to burn it or bury it, but her goes nearly mad when I tells her so, and arguifies about it. 'You'd be burning or burying me, our dad,' her says. 'You mustn't do that. Only find out who's doing it,' her says, 'and then I can wish it back on 'em, whoever it is, and wish the curse away.' "

"Is your daughter married?"

"No, her beant, but her's promised to Walter Oddley, and have been, these past eight year. But her don't like to leave me, you see. Got nobody else, I haven't. Pity they didn't put the witchcraft on me, and get me out of the way. More of a burden not a father, but what can I do? I can't force her out of the house, and there's beant room for three."

"Hasn't her man got a cottage?"

"No. He lodges with Mrs. Smithers. Have done, this last 12 year."

"Where's your village?"

"Tall Steeple."

"And people there still believe in witches? Well, well! I'm afraid I don't know how to advise you. I should call in the doctor, however, whether your daughter likes it or not."

She nodded, smiled without mirth or friendliness, and joined her chauffeur.

"We must postpone the rest of our inspection, George," she said. "We have a case of attempted murder to investigate. Drive me at once to Tall Steeple."

×

Inquiry at the only shop in Tall Steeple elicited the fact that Walter Oddley lodged at the second cottage past the church and, leaving George in charge of the car which he parked at the church gate, Mrs. Bradley went to the cottage and found a middle-aged woman doing the washing. She was assisted by a bright and comely girl of about 20 years of age.

"Walt? He be working," said the woman. "Be off about 12 and back here for his dinner. And that reminds me, Hester," she added to the girl, "you best put on the tatties, else they won't get done. Did ee want to see Walt special?" she went on, addressing Mrs. Bradley with naive confidence.

"Yes, I did. I am the specialist he has called in to examine his fiancée, who, I understand, is ill," said Mrs. Bradley mendaciously.

"Oh, that there Jane Symes, poor creetur! Oh ah, her've been laid up some time now. But Walt never said nowt about calling in any specialist. I should have thought he'd have told me.

"Well, seeing you've come, you'd best go along and see the poor thing, I suppose, if Walt sent for ee. But I *do* think he might have been open. We been pretty good friends all these years."

"I was hoping to have a talk with him first, and that he would conduct me to the house."

"Well, ee can't miss it. Last one, standing by itself, at the end of the common."

She pointed. Mrs. Bradley thanked her and went back to the car. In a minute or two she was standing outside a small cottage with a long front garden. She walked up the path, took the doorkey from a nail in the porch, opened the door and went upstairs.

The woman in the bed was emaciated to the point of extinction.

"Yes?" she said in a whisper.

"I am the spell to end all spells," said Mrs. Bradley in her deep and beautiful voice. "Who is doing this to you?"

"I don't know." The large eyes closed wearily.

"Well, we'll soon find out," said Mrs. Bradley, under her breath. She went softly out of the room. Downstairs, in the cupboard under the stairs, she found the corn-baby. It was like the museum exhibits except for one particular. Stuck through its plaited stomach were two large black-headed pins.

Mrs. Bradley impounded the horrid little object, went out of the cottage, locking the door and hanging the key up again, and returned to her car. She bade George drive to the village shop. Here she purchased tin-tacks, a bundle of firewood and a ball of thin string, and returned with these items to the car.

"George," she said. "Have you a strong penknife?"

"Yes, madam."

"Good. Let us drive on to the common, which I see is well-wooded, and there, safe from prying eyes, we'll do and we'll do and we'll do."

George recognised the quotation, and, understanding his employer's personality, permitted himself a grim smile.

"What did you wish me to do, madam, when we achieve the common?"

"I want you to construct a gallows, George."

"Very good, madam. Out of the bundle of wood?"

"Indeed, yes. How intelligent you are."

×

The common was indeed well-wooded. The car crept on up a green lane and embedded itself among trees. George pulled up and, guided by his employer and aided by the tin-tacks, the thin string and the wood, created a presentable gallows on which Mrs. Bradley hung the corn-baby with success and rather horrible effect.

"There!" said Mrs. Bradley, surveying their efforts with satisfaction. "I think that should do very nicely."

They drove sedately back into the village, and, at Mrs. Bradley's orders, to Mr. Symes's house. As she had assumed, the old man was home by this time, and opened the door at her knock. He looked astounded when he realised who had called.

"You, ma'am? Indebted, I'm sure! What can I do for ee now?"

"You can tell your daughter to get up."

"But the poor gal — "

"I know. You tell her what I say, there's a good man. If you don't know what I'm talking about, go and look in the cupboard under the stairs."

Mystified, he went along to look and came back wide-eyed.

"You came here and snuck it," he said. Mrs. Bradley gravely agreed, and waited for him to say more.

"And where do you keep the weed-killer?" she demanded, when it was clear that he was not going to speak.

"Weed-killer?"

"Yes, where is it? Didn't you know your daughter is being poisoned?"

"Poisoned? I know her mind be poisoned. What can I do about that?"

"Obviously nothing. Just tell her that the spell is removed."

"But be it removed?"

"Look here, Mr. Symes," said Mrs. Bradley impatiently, "do you believe in spells, or do you not?"

He looked dimly and doubtfully at her. "I wouldn't say one way or t'other," he announced.

"Right. Then we know where we are. I shall be along again to your house very shortly."

For a threat it was couched in dulcet tones, but as a threat alone he regarded it.

"You don't need to blame me," he muttered. Mrs. Bradley made no response to this, except to say in her ordinary manner:

"That settles everything. Are you prepared to insist that your daughter break her engagement?"

"Break her engagement? Oh, but her'll never do that! Where ud she find another? Her's rising thirty-six year old. Happen I did ought to go into a home or sommat. I dunno."

Mrs. Bradley left him and drove to the cottage in which Walt Oddley lodged. He was having his dinner and it seemed unfair to interrupt him, so she went back and sat in the car and nursed George's neat piece of woodwork.

x

Walt came outside, sat on the front step of the cottage and lighted a pipe. He was a man of about forty, good-looking and well set-up. Mentally Mrs. Bradley contrasted his sun-tanned skin and capable great hands with the anemic creature near to the point of death in Symes's little cottage.

She walked up the garden path, and without a word, put the little wooden gallows, from which the corn-baby dangled so horribly, down beside him. He looked owlishly from the exhibit into her snapping black eyes. Then he pitched forward with a groan. Mrs. Bradley waited for him to come round.

"Yes," she said, when he had recovered. "Sweet and twenty may be preferable to six and thirty. How did you give her the weed-killer?"

"In gravy cubes," he answered huskily. "I made her promise to drink a drop of gravy every day. I never meant to finish her off, only to make her sickly so I'd got an excuse not to wed with her. She thought it was *that*," he pointed to the dangling corn-baby, "so, of course, she never suspicioned. You going to tell the police?"

"I don't know. She would have died, you know, if I hadn't come along and found you out. I knew it was either you or her father. But her father, if he didn't want her to marry, would have put the corn-baby — and the arsenic — in your way, not in hers, and when I saw your landlady's daughter I was certain which way the wind blew."

"What be I going to do now?"

"Together she and I will watch you shred the corn-baby into little tiny bits. But we'd better dismantle the gallows. This time I hope they won't be needed."

A Bit of Garden

It was a bit of luck for Timms to get the bottom end of Lucast's garden.

The ground was pretty clear of weed and easy to dig. Timms knew the soil was good, and the whole garden had been well looked after. There were fruit trees and raspberry canes in the part nearest the house, so Timms and his labours were pretty well screened off and interfered with nobody. He felt he had almost as much privacy as if the garden had been his own.

Timms had soon broken the news to his wife and, for the first time in 12 years, found himself mildly approved of.

"We'll have our own new potatoes, peas, beans, onions, carrots, lettuces, parsley, mint, turnips, parsnips. Brussels sprouts, curly kale, marrows, rhubarb — " he began. Mrs. Timms sniffed doubtfully.

"I shall get up at six," said Timms happily, "and get the bit of garden all ship-shape, Lucast won't know the place, come this time a fortnight, I bet."

"There's no reason why he should. And while you're about it you can take some cuttings from these carnations and put them in. They make nice flowers for the house, and they're overcrowded in that little front garden."

×

Timms did not want carnations among his vegetables, but he knew better than to say so.

Before he had finished the digging, the carnations were safely bedded at the end of the plot, ready to be broken up and planted out when he had made up his mind where to put them.

He tackled the digging with great goodwill, and when Good Friday came he was up at dawn ready to plant his potatoes. He calculated that he would be able to have the whole morning to himself away from his wife, her acid tongue and her everlasting schemes for finding him work about the house. He was disappointed.

You can't go trapesing off to that place to-day. Mother and Auntie are coming, and I want you — "

"I'm going to get my spuds in," he retorted.

"If you dare to go out of this house except to meet Mother and Auntie at the station, and bring them here on the bus, I'll never speak to you again, Albert Timms."

He squirmed and inwardly raged, but he had given in too often and over too long a time to be able to defy and defeat her now.

×

The visit of the elderly relatives passed off without incident.

When, several days later, he managed to get home from work a bit earlier than usual and was sneaking out of the back gate with his seed potatoes and a dibber, he was astounded to find his wife grimly waiting outside the house.

"I'm coming to see where I want you to put my carnations. Those potatoes will do any old time," she told him firmly.

He put down the sack and stared at her.

"Look here, Millie, the carnations won't come to any harm. They're planted all right. You could put them out yourself as you want them, any time during the day while I'm at work. But I *must* get the spuds in, dear, else we shan't get any nice little new potatoes later on."

"I'm going to see my carnations put in properly. You can take that old sack back indoors. By the time the carnations are done you won't have time to plant potatoes to-night, not at *your* rate of crawling about."

×

He humped the sack higher on his back and trudged off in the direction of Lucast's bit of garden. But although for once he had asserted himself — for she did not attempt to follow him, but went back into the house — his pleasure was spoilt.

Time passed and the potatoes began to shoot. Timms was happy and proud. He was going to get a fine crop.

"I must hoe up those spuds," he said to his wife. "Quite time they were trenched. I'll do it to-night when I've been home and had my tea. The light lasts longer now we've got summer time back."

As it happened, he went there before going home to his tea, just for the pleasure of looking at the dark green plants. The devastation which met his eyes seemed to him as dreadful as a massacre. He stared incredulously at the wrecked garden, and then his eye caught the carnations. He turned and went home. For the second time since his marriage he had made up his mind.

"You'd better come along with me after tea, Millie," he said quietly. "More than time we set out them carnations of yours. They've been on my mind ever since I put in my potatoes."

"If you're going to do that as well as hoe up your potatoes, you'd better be getting along," she told him.

"I rather wanted my tea."

"You'll have to go on wanting. If you're going to do the carnations, I certainly want to see what you're up to with them."

What she really wanted, he knew, was to be present when he saw his wrecked garden and to point out to him the folly of disobeying her. He shrugged his shoulders — a thing he had never dared to do before — and picked up the hoe and the small fork and trowel.

×

"Funny case," said Detective-inspector Trammles. "We were absolutely positive he'd made away with her. Had reason, too, poor devil, from what we could hear.

"But we couldn't find out where he'd put her, and if he'd only let well alone he might be a free man this day instead of awaiting trial.

"His story was that they both went down to this bit of garden he rented, and when they'd finished the job he'd planned for that evening — setting out some carnations it was — he called in at the local and she went home to cook some fish.

"He called us up next morning and reported that she hadn't been at home when he got there and hadn't come back all night.

"We made some enquiries, of course, and very soon saw how the land lay. It wasn't a secret that his life was next door to hell. Besides, someone had wrecked his potato plot, and, according to the chap who lives in the house — respectable type, name of Lucast — ran for the Council last year — she was the only person besides Timms himself who could have got hold of the key to the back gate and gone down there.

"Motive enough for murder, that wrecked potato plot, we reckoned. I can just imagine if *my* missus — but then, of course, she wouldn't.

"Well, as I say, we had our suspicions from the start, but not being able to find the body or the weapon, we were helpless. He'd planted out the carnations all right, so of course, we had them all up and dug deep.

"Then we dug all the rest of the garden. Nothing. Just not a thing. After a week or two Timms came along and asked if he could have the use of the plot again. There wasn't any reason to refuse him. Very shortly afterwards we arrested and charged him.

" 'I don't see how you got on to it,' " he said to me. Nice little chap as you'd wish to meet, and he seemed more surprised than upset to think we'd rumbled him.

" 'No,' I told him. 'I don't suppose you do, but you've got to get up very early in the morning to stall us off for very long, you know.

" 'You stabbed her through the ear with your little gardening fork, didn't you? Then you put the body in the sack you used for your seed potatoes and humped it away and hid it while we did what you thought we'd do — dug over the whole of your bit of garden down at Mr. Lucast's place.

" 'But, when you went back to that garden, you left such an obvious clue that we couldn't ignore it.'

" 'I wish I knew what it was,' he said, honestly puzzled. 'Why .should you go back and dig up my garden again? You'd been all over it once. I thought it would be such a very good place to move her to, and I wanted to bury her decent.'

" 'Yes, but, you see, old chap,' I said, 'we'd been over that garden so thoroughly, and dug it so deep, that we couldn't make out why you dug all over again. In fact, there was only one reason, and we found it, didn't we?'

"He came quietly, and he's been quiet and resigned ever since. His wife was a she-devil. Justifiable homicide, I'd, call it, if I was on the jury. *I've* got potatoes in, too!"

The Swimming Gala

When it all came out at the trial there was no doubt the murder had been planned.

Mind you, it turned out that tongues had begun to wag as soon as young Smith and his sister had been appointed as deputy superintendents at our Public Baths, especially as old Ford, the Baths Superintendent, had had no say in the appointments. The girl was to take over the ticket office — adults ninepence, children under fifteen fourpence — and the young chap acted as instructor, mopper-up, and assistant chucker-out of louts.

Both were good swimmers, especially the lad, and he made no bones about telling the Baths Committee that he was only going to stay until he had mastered the job. He wanted a Baths of his own. This was none too satisfactory from our point of view, but you've got to take what you can get in these days, especially as the pay isn't any too good, and the brother and sister seemed a well-spoken young couple and the lad's qualifications were first class.

x

The couple had been appointed in April, and in the following September the Swimming Club held its annual gala. The men and women members held their club practices on different days of the week, but joined forces for the gala and finished up with a mixed team race — two men and two girls on each side. This was the high spot of the evening.

Well, the first I knew of anything being wrong was when my chauffeur came into the Mayor's Parlour and held out an envelope.

"Found on the floor of the interior compartment of the mayoral car, Mr. Mayor, sir, when I was cleaning her for tonight's do."

Tonight's do happened to be a parent-teacher gathering at the local grammar school, and I was not looking forward to it much. There is something about those BA and MA hoods and gowns that makes me feel I left school at the age of twelve unable to read and write. Besides, the chairman of the parents happened to be the man who thought he ought to have been mayor that year.

x

Putting aside these thoughts, I opened the envelope.

"You ought to keep your eyes and ears open," the letter read, "but I supposed you can't swim. Don't you know what's going on under your silly old beak? I supposed you take your something bath at home, if any."

It was unsigned, of course. I'm not proud. I showed it to the chauffeur. After all, we had gone to the same primary school.

"What do you make of it?" I asked. To my surprise he looked rather uncomfortable.

"There's been rumours, Mr. Mayor, sir."

"What about? Me?"

"No, about the public baths, sir. Bit of a scandal, it seems."

"There's always some rumour about the public baths, and has been ever since we allowed mixed bathing."

"That's not it this time, Mr. Mayor, sir. This isn't general, it's particular."

"Well, get on with it. What do you know?" The mayor's chauffeur, hanging about for hours and hours during every municipal function, is the repository of most of the gossip that's going, as well I knew. "Come on, Henry, let's have it."

"Well, Ted, as man to man I don't exactly know anything, but I can tell you what's going about. There's a sort of fussation about young Bob Smith at the baths."

"But why? The attendance has bucked up no end since he came, and he's taken over the coaching for the swimming club and made a good job of it, so I hear. Doesn't he behave himself with the ladies?"

"It's with one particular lady, Ted — his sister. It's said she's not his sister and she isn't his wife, neither."

"Oh, good heavens. Even if the fellow's a Mormon it doesn't make any difference to his job. It's the usual pussies making the usual mischief."

"Some councilors didn't ought to have wives," said Henry. "But, all the same, you know, Ted, there's no smoke without fire."

"Now what do you mean by that?"

"I heard it put about as the chairman of the Baths Committee would like to get rid of poor old Ford and give the job to Smith and his sister so as to keep them here."

×

Well, the Splash Night came, and Henry drove me and the mayoress to the baths. There was the usual bouquet for her and the usual interval speech for me so that the swimmers could get a breather while I was making it, and then came the high spots — the dying competition and the mixed team race.

It was during the latter, when every eye was fixed on the swimmers and you couldn't hear a thing except the din, that a shot was fired and the chairman of the Baths Committee fell dead into the water.

Perhaps I ought to explain the geography of the swimming baths. You enter the building by turnstile and then there are two ways in. Either you charge in at the first doors and find a dressing box — that's the procedure if you've come for a swim — or else you walk along a corridor behind the men's side of the bath and come to the slipper baths, where you get the soap and water caper if you haven't a bathroom at home.

You also come to some swing doors which open on to the deep end of the swimming bath almost opposite the diving boards.

Through this door the murderer had come, and had picked off the victim, who was standing on the opposite side of the bath helping to judge the team race. A child of ten couldn't have missed.

The only clue, if you can call it that, was the Baths Superintendent's overcoat, hat and gloves which the police found, together with the revolver, chucked down in the passage outside, which at that time must have been empty, for everyone was watching the race.

There were no prints on the gun, of course, because of the gloves, and the whole thing turned on a question of motive. Two people only were involved, it seemed, and their motives were completely dissimilar. It appeared for a time as though the only person who could have given a casting vote was the man lying dead in the parish mortuary, to which he had been taken after young Smith had dived in and fished him out of the water.

What it came to was this: either old Ford, the bath's superintendent, had shot to save his job, or young Smith had fired to try to keep himself out of prison, for the couple turned out not only to be married but to be bigamously married. But nobody seemed to know whether the dead councilor had known this.

However, the police arrested Smith on the bigamy charge, and then went on investigating the murder. I went into a huddle with them, with the Baths Committee and with the full Council, but nobody seemed able to help.

The chief trouble was that nobody had been able to give a description of the murderer owing to the interest that was taken in the team race, and the overcoat and hat were not in themselves enough to incriminate Ford, as his house adjoined the Baths and had been left unlocked as it always was unless he went into the town.

×

To cut the cackle, young Smith was hanged. The police were able to prove that nobody left the Baths directly after the shot was fired, and that nobody except the officials had used the corridor which was reserved on gala nights for them and for some of the swimmers who were using the slipper baths as dressing-rooms, and these swimmers and officials were all on the Bath level at the time.

Smith had put on the overcoat over bathing trunks, done the deed, flung off coat, hat, and gloves and tossed down the revolver.

Then all he had to do was to dash to the rescue of the body just to emphasize the way he was dressed or undressed, if you prefer it. When the police charged him he confessed, and admitted that the dead councilor had known of the bigamous marriage and was threatening to expose him.

Who worked it all out and presented his conclusions to the police? I did.

The Tooth-Pick

We had the story from a chap called Bongo. I don't know his real name; it was almost impossible to pronounce and I never saw it spelt. He was some sort of foreigner, of course. You could tell that from his appearance, let alone his name.

Besides, an Englishman would never have had such a hobby, I'm perfectly sure ... or, if he had, I don't believe he would have told a roomful of people all about it, especially when ladies were present.

"My hobby," he said, "is the collecting of cocktail sticks, and, owing to a fortunate circumstance, which I will detail in a moment, my collection happens to be unique. There is nothing to match it anywhere."

"Not even in America?" said someone. Bongo shook his head and smiled.

"Not even in America," he said. "To explain: I had a friend (he is dead now) who was prison dentist at Sfor. You won't know Sfor. You won't find it on the map. It lies in the heart of Mlong, and only very bad men are sent there, and, unless they're hanged, they are all lifers. All the same, the prison conditions are not too bad; and the men get good medical attention and there is always a resident dentist.

"Now my friend was a peculiar sort of fellow, or he would never have taken such a job, for he was in no sort of trouble, legal, matrimonial or otherwise. After a bit he began to get rather bored. So he invented an occupation.

"This occupation depended upon the willing co-operation of the convicts (for my friend would never deliberately take advantage of them), but most of them would do most things for five shillings ... the currency was not in English money really, but that gives the approximate value ... because they always wanted to buy tobacco, which they were allowed to do if they had sufficient dough."

"You mean he gave them five bob if they didn't go cowardly on him in the dentist's chair?" asked Tompkins, who was known to be having all his teeth out shortly.

"Bravery did not enter into it, in a sense," replied Bongo. "If a convict's teeth needed doing, they were done. No; my friend simply asked them (when he'd got them in the chair) whether, for five shillings, they would allow him to extract one sound tooth, which he said he would like to keep as a memento. Most of them fell for it, of course, because of the money, which he paid each time on the nail.

x

"Well, time passed, and while it had been passing my friend had occupied himself, evening after evening, by crowning little sharp spikes of elephant ivory with the convicts' sound teeth until he had the germ and the gem of my present collection.

"He was extremely pleased with it, but unfortunately he caught fever and died. He had left me the things in his will, together with a full tally of the convicts from whom the teeth had been taken. In due course the collection came to me from the prison governor. I have taken pleasure and pride in adding to it, but, of course, no such wonderful specimen ever came my way again."

"I daresay that your collection, because of this nucleus of tooth-topped pieces, is unique and probably unmatchable," said Smith, "but what about the murder you promised us?"

"All in good time," replied Bongo. "I am coming to the murder immediately. It so happens that after I received this precious legacy of the cocktail sticks I got to know a man called Gobbo. I only call him that because his first name was Lancelot, and it would not do for me to tell you his real name, for a reason that you will understand in a minute.

"This Gobbo was a doctor, and some time after we had become acquainted he introduced me to a pal of his named Locksley. I call him Locksley because his great interest was archery and he was always preaching the advantages of the sport ... equally suited to both sexes (he was a great man for the ladies), open-air pastime, no foot-slogging such as in golf, or aimless rushing about and getting hurt, as in rugby football.

"Whenever he made what he called a convert he would invite the convert and other devotees to his flat and stand them drinks. He was a bachelor, by the way, so there was no obstructive missus to be placated if the party got a trifle out of hand.

"Well, one day Gobbo met me at our usual rendezvous and asked me what I would have. I named it and we settled down to our usual game of draughts. When I was getting up to go for the second round, he said, 'No, no, old man. My shout.' And he went to the bar and called for the same again, which happened to be double brandies.

" 'What is it? Your birthday or something?' I inquired. Presently it appeared that Gobbo wanted me to do him a favour. 'There's a fellow I particularly want to impress,' he said, 'and that fellow happens to be Locksley. He's been asked to send a team of three archers to the County Tournament, and I'm the fourth best long-bowman in his outfit. Now if only he could be persuaded that I was the third best ... '

" 'Well, you'll have to practise,' I pointed out, 'and reduce your handicap or whatever it is.' But it appeared that he thought little of this suggestion. The names had to go in at the end of the week so that the programmes could be printed.

"At last he got to the point. I was to act as host to himself, Locksley and two of the toxophilists. I was to bring out my tooth-topped cocktail-sticks. We would all get fearfully tight ... or, anyhow, see that Locksley did ... and all the drinks would be on Gobbo. It was to be no expense to me, but he did want to use my flat and it was essential that he should have my special cocktail-sticks.

" 'But I never use them!' I cried. 'They're simply curios, that's all.'

"However, he would not take no for an answer, and after two more double brandies, both out of his pocket, I decided that I couldn't very well be curmudgeonly about the things.

×

"Well, the evening came and the party began. There were the five of us. The others were numbers one and three of the proposed archery team, Locksley rating himself (quite justly, according to Gobbo), as number two.

"I may as well admit, here and now, that Gobbo never betrayed the slightest animosity against the man. There was food ... sandwiches and snacks, including walnuts and salted almonds ... and everything went with a swing.

"I produced my convict cocktail sticks and told, I flatter myself, a pretty good story about them. Meanwhile I noticed that Locksley, who was getting slightly tight, was cramming into the salted almonds for all he was worth, and if he faltered Gobbo plied him again and again and Locksley never said no.

"Then Gobbo handed out the next round and in each glass, stuck into an olive, was a convict's toothpick, as Gobbo laughingly called it. The nuts and the word toothpick apparently connected in Locksley's mind, for after he had eaten his olive he began to use the cocktail stick to clean his molars.

"He must have pricked himself rather badly ... he let out a curse anyway, and dropped the cocktail stick on to the floor. I never saw it again. Gobbo bent and picked it up and I was not so far over as not to be able to see that he slipped it into his waistcoat pocket.

"I couldn't say anything then, but I thought I would jog his memory when it was time to break up the party. As it happened, I didn't. Matters got a bit steamy and I forgot.

"Locksley died of tetanus. When I counted my toothpicks ... I mean my cocktail sticks ... I still had the original number. I know Gobbo put one in his waistcoat pocket. I know I never saw it again. I know Gobbo was a doctor with a chance of obtaining cultures of anthrax.

×

"I don't know why he should want to make an end of Locksley ... it couldn't have been the archery competition ... but there it is."

"You must have seen double ... about Gobbo putting one of the tooth — er — cocktail sticks into his pocket," said someone.

"I might believe so," said Bongo, nodding. "Yes, I quite see your point, sir. But I happen to be a dentist, like my friend who left me his collection, and Gobbo made an appointment for an extraction. There was only the root left in of the tooth he showed me.

" 'How come?' " I asked jocularly, although my stomach went cold.

" 'Pulled it out myself. It was loose,' he answered; and he looked me full in the eye."

The Bodkin

"The trouble with the English language," said Calkin, "is that there are too many words which don't mean the same thing. Take the case of John and Molly, for example."

"John and Molly Who?" asked Scond.

"That is immaterial. This John and Molly ... or, rather, these John and Molly, as Scond here is a purist for grammar ... were an apparently happy and devoted young couple, but to those of us who knew them the worm entered the wheat after the first three rehearsals of the village play.

"The trouble was a woman named Lally ... Alice, I suppose she'd been christened, but Lally was how she was known. This woman was somebody's niece and not a local resident, but because she was an ex-RADA she was given the chief part in my play."

"*Your* play?" asked Scond, raising his eyebrows.

"Yes. We'd struck a slight deficit the year before, and the committee decided to rely on a non-royalty production to try and square things up. The company objected to dipping into their jeans to balance the books. So I offered to toss them off a light, witty trifle needing only one set and modern dress, but when I got down to it, it seemed a bit tedious like that, so I had three sets, one for each act, and period costume ... George III you know ... in which everybody looks handsome.

"Well, we rehearsed in mufti, of course, except for Lally. She said it ruined her art to speak words like Odds my life, and ... "

"Young women didn't say Odds my life. It's an oath," said Scond.

"The young woman in my play did. She was the daughter of the squire, a hot-blooded old Tory who cared neither for man nor devil, and the girl took after him. She dressed mostly in a full-skirted riding-habit of Lincoln green, and wore a black tricorne hat trimmed with gold, and she was apt to slash would-be suitors across the face with her riding-switch.

"It was a peach of a part, and Lally insisted on dressing up for it at every rehearsal. Very fine she looked, too, and there was soon no doubt that John, who was leading man and who tamed her and married her in the third act, was fully aware of the fact, and soon began to signify same in the usual manner.

"Molly was livid, of course. For one thing, she had coveted Lally's part for herself, and might have got it but for Lally, and, for another, she realised, sooner than we did, that her John was being led astray.

×

"Now I mustn't put the cart before the horse, because that would spoil the story, so I will pass now to the fair which came to our village somewhere about mid-way of the rehearsals for the play. This fair was an annual institution, but this time it put up a new feature ... a fortune teller. She was an ancient dame, picturesquely bearded, and she inhabited a small modern caravan on the edge of the fairground.

"As soon as I saw this caravan and read Squaw Chipmunk Tee-pee-wee's lurid advertisement, I knew that there was only one thing for me to do. I charged into that caravan and produced my half-crown.

"I had my money's worth all right. The crone began a bit stickily, but she warmed up pretty soon and got on to the subject of my play. She didn't seem to tumble to it that it was merely for amateurs. She described it as a work of genius and foretold that I should make a fortune out of it."

"Of course, I knew better, but I affected pleasure at her prophecy, and then she got on to the real stuff.

"She began to get very close to the bone anent those two girls, Molly and Lally. She spoke of ruin coming to my play because of a bodkin, and she added that the said bodkin would be wielded by somebody called Mally ... not Molly, mind you, and not Lally. Simply Mally, which might have been either of them.

"Evil would come of a bodkin, she repeated, and the only way to forestall the evil would be to give up the play, and this she earnestly begged me to do."

"But, of course, you could scarcely be expected to do that, with this fortune coming to you from it," said Scond, sarcastically. Calkin ignored him again, and continued.

"I did give her another half-crown, as a matter of fact, and asked her to tell me more, but she shuddered and shook her elf-locks ... "

"You can only have one elf-lock," said Scond.

"She had several," Calkin insisted, "and she shook them all. What's more, she returned my second half-crown, which, in itself, should have caused me to smell a rat, but all I thought at the time was that she suspected it to be a bad one. It wasn't, though, I changed it for a stout and mild that same evening at the Goat and Grapes, and the barman didn't even bounce it. To cut a long story short ... "

×

"Thank heaven for that," said Scond.

"To cut a long story short, I told the crowd at rehearsal next day that I had been warned to take off the play, but, of course, they only laughed, and, as it happened, the rehearsal went particularly well, and I soon forgot the gipsy's warning. The duelling scene where the heroine, dressed as a man ... "

"I thought she always wore a riding-habit of Lincoln green and a black tricorne hat trimmed with gold," said Scond.

"She was dressed as a man to aid her in escaping from her father's ancestral hall," said Calkin firmly, "and was involved in a duel with her lover, who, of course, mistook her for his rival to her hand and heart.

"Well, up to that time I had been unable to get John to put any spirit into his performance in this scene. He was too much afraid of hurting Lally, he said. I got a bit fed-up with the poor chap, I remember, and several times urged him to pep himself up and make the thing look life-like.

"On this occasion he certainly did. It turned out that there had been more than a bit of a breeze between him and Molly before they set out for the rehearsal, and he was emotionally disturbed.

"Lally was quite out of breath at the end of the scene, and more than a bit peevish. She accused him of playing too rough, and John apologized, with one eye on Molly, and promised to go lighter with her next time, but I wasn't going to have my play spoiled because of any silly scruples of that sort. I praised them both to the skies and persuaded Lally that her artistic conscience was at stake."

"It couldn't be," said Scond. "You can't have your conscience at stake, only your honour."

"It was nothing to do with her honour. Don't be coarse," said Calkin. "Her artistic conscience, I repeat, was at stake, and so I told her. I carried my point, too, and she arranged to practise daily with John to get the duel the high-spot of the play, as I had always contended that it should be.

"The idea that her John and this Lally were to meet for daily private rehearsals got right under Molly's skin. However, there was nothing she could do about it except to muscle in at the first rehearsal.

"Lally complained. I upheld this. It was doing the scene no good to have Lally put off her stroke by a sour-faced young woman who sat and sewed up jumpers with a large bodkin. I don't mind telling you that it gave me a jittery feeling when I heard of this bodkin, because of the fortune-teller's warning. I'm a superstitious bloke and ... "

"Yes, you told us," said Scond.

"Anyway, after Lally complained I asked Molly to put the bodkin away and I indicated that if she could keep herself away, too, it wouldn't do the rehearsals any harm. She promised, but it wasn't any good. The accident happened just the same."

"Accident?" said Scond. "I thought it was supposed to be a murder."

"It was. It murdered my play. The dress rehearsal came, and no John. Molly said that he was ill, but it proved later that he had got himself locked in the coal-hole. His understudy didn't know the part, and in the end we put Molly into the costume as she'd rehearsed John in his words and knew them backwards.

"It was in the duelling scene, of course, that things broke loose. Someone had taken the buttons off the foils. We could never bring it home to Molly, but there didn't seem much doubt."

"She *killed* her rival!" exclaimed Scond. Calkin shook his head.

"She'd have liked to, I dare say, but it didn't get as far as that. She damaged her, though and pretty nastily. The play was doomed, of course. We couldn't put it on after that. But, you see, the fortune-teller proved to be right. She said disaster would come through a bodkin, and it did. Remember Hamlet? *With a bare bodkin?*"

"But bodkin meant a dagger or a sword, in those days," said Scond. "Oh, of course! And the fortune-teller had been Molly got up in disguise, I suppose?"

"How did you know that?" asked Calkin, smirking a little.

"Because it's as phoney as the rest of the story," said Scond.

The Boxer

"That dog's a fool," Battling Bert Billcaster said to his wife. "I thought he was trained as a guard-dog!"

"Why, what's the matter, Bert?"

"The matter is," said the Battler crossly, "that instead of doing his job he let himself be kept quiet with a chunk of horseflesh — I found the bone in his kennel — while chicken thieves raided the hen-house and helped themselves to a couple of my prize Buff Orpingtons."

"Oh, dear. I'm ever so sorry. You said you wanted a guard-dog for those silver cups of yours, so I went over to those kennels at Monkshurst Hill. They wanted me to take a puppy but I wouldn't, because of what you said. He came with a lovely pedigree, and he's a real nice dog."

She spoke wistfully. She longed for her tough husband's approval and affection and seemed unable to win either. For months, she knew, he had been going with that barmaid down at the Duke's Head.

"That dog," went on Billcaster darkly, "would let us all get murdered, if you ask me, sooner than trouble himself to raise a bark."

"Give him a chance, Bert, dear. He's new to the place as yet."

×

No more was said at the time, but, somewhat to Mrs. Billcaster's surprise, her husband began to make a fuss of the dog. He named it Sullivan. He even sent her to the library to get a book on boxers to learn how best to train and feed them.

Day after day Billcaster, who was in training for one of the minor bouts by which he got a living, would take the dog out on road-work or play with him in the field behind the house. But three weeks later Sullivan again failed to prevent a burglary. Before he turned professional, the Battler had been a promising amateur and had won several silver cups and a belt. They were kept in a case on the sideboard, were greatly admired by visitors, and had always made Mrs. Billcaster nervous about burglars.

One morning she came downstairs as usual to light the fire so that her husband could have a cheerful breakfast and, to her horror, she saw the desecrated cabinet. Every silver trophy was gone.

×

She ran to the foot of the stairs and called out hysterically to her husband to come down and see what had happened. He gave one look at the top of the sideboard, said morosely, "I *thought* I heard somebody shuffling about last night. That's why I hopped out of bed and came down to investigate. Remember?"

"I know. You were a long time, too. But you never saw anyone, did you?"

"No, but I made a search. Put my match gloves on, too. I'd have been sorry for the ... if I'd copped him."

"Yes, so would I, Bert. You'll go for the police, I suppose?"

"No, I shan't. Where's that fool of a dog of yours? I'll teach him his business, that's what I'll do. Why should I lose my tin because of him?"

"Oh, don't hit him, Bert. You'll break his back." He went out, tied the dog up and thrashed him savagely. The next day he went to take the dog out as usual, but the dog looked at him and growled, not loudly but with such unmistakable menace that the man left him tied up and went to do his road-work alone.

When he had gone the woman approached the dog. He accepted food from her but would not allow her to let him off the chain and take him out. When he came back from his road-work, Billcaster appeared to have regained his temper and went out to play with Sullivan, but the dog would have nothing to do with him.

The Battler laughed and told his wife that he had gone to the police, after all, about the theft of his trophies and that they might come to the house next day. But next day his wife was dead. He came home from his bout (he had lost) to find his wife, with her neck broken, lying out in the middle of the lawn.

The police appeared, summoned by Billcaster at once. They made their investigation, took photographs and fingerprints, and promised to come back on the following day.

"Funny about that dog," said the sergeant to the inspector. "You'd have thought he'd have given tongue, wouldn't you, if anyone attacked his mistress?"

"Funny about the dog all through," said the inspector. "According to Billcaster's evidence, the dog let the chickens be stolen, he let the cups be stolen, and he let the wife be murdered, all, apparently, without making a sound. It's the old Sherlock Holmes Silver Blaze gag about the dog that did nothing in the nighttime."

"You mean Billcaster stole his own fowls and his own cups, sir? And then murdered his wife, hoping we'd think it was burglars?"

"Well," said the inspector, "what do you think?"

×

It was just possible, according to the medical evidence, that Mrs. Billcaster could have been murdered at just about the time when her husband set out for the boxing ring. On the other hand, she might not have died until halfway through his bout.

Billcaster said that his wife never went to see him fight. She could not bear to think that he might be knocked about. He had said good-bye to her, as usual, at the front door, and had arrived home later to find her dead. He said that he supposed it must have been burglars. He explained again about the loss of the Buff Orpingtons and his silver trophies. They asked him why he had not called in the police as soon as the burglaries took place. Billcaster waved his hand. They surely must understand how it was. He did not like to go to the police. He had never been mixed up with the police, like, and did not want to begin.

But if he had only known how it would go with poor old Ethel, well, he would have passed up on every fight in the world, sooner than have left her with only that fool of a dog.

×

The police asked him about the barmaid at the Duke's Head. "She says," declared the inspector, "that you admitted paternity and said you would see her right." Billcaster snarled: "She's got an imagination!" was all he said.

Then the inspector asked for the services of a police-constable who was said to be a wonder with dogs. This young man had had a police dog in his charge for a year and a half.

"The evidence is," the inspector told him, "that, although prize chickens and prize cups and a silver boxing belt were removed, the dog did nothing and the thefts were not reported to us. My inference is that Billcaster planned to murder his wife and thought of a plan which he put into operation by hiding his own property in the hope that we should believe the murder was the work of cosh thieves.

"Now, according to the neighbours (when trouble turns up, they are usually reliable witnesses, you know) Billcaster treated the dog well, took him out, fed him himself, and made quite a fuss of him, even after the fowls disappeared.

"But (still according to the neighbours) after the theft of his cups and belt Billcaster thrashed the dog and spoilt his temper. Then, almost immediately afterwards, the wife was found murdered. I fancy she must have been killed indoors, then taken into the garden. It's too much to expect that the dog would not have given tongue if a struggle went on in front of his kennel. Well, see what you can do."

×

The young man went and looked at Sullivan; he spoke to him; but the dog backed and growled.

"Untie him," he said to Billcaster. "He's used to you."

But as soon as Billcaster approached the dog grew so savage that he backed away. "I don't like a dog as can't take a hiding," he said. "But you can see what it is. He'll have the throat out of me if I touch him."

"Well, he'll have to come off the chain some time. He can't spend the rest of his life chained up. Where did you buy him?"

But it was Mrs. Billcaster who had made the purchase, and although the police searched the house they found no record of the transaction.

"All right," said the constable, "I suggest we advertise. Mrs. Billcaster would have given her name at the kennels. Even if, for any reason, she didn't, we've only to check on the breeders of boxer dogs."

The breeder, traced without much trouble, turned out to be a middle-aged woman. She had not wanted to part with Sullivan she said, but Mrs. Billcaster had refused to consider a puppy and Sullivan had so far proved unsatisfactory at mating, so reluctantly, she had sold him.

She was brought to Billcaster's house. The dog recognised her at once, and with such pleasure that she offered to buy him back, but Billcaster would have nothing to do with the offer. He went back into his house.

"Well," said the constable to the breeder, "now that you're here, Miss Evans, I think we can trust him. I'm going to let him off the chain."

×

The constable talked to the dog and then set him free. He patted him and, still talking cheerfully, knelt and peered into the kennel. The next moment he was knocked violently sideways. The dog stood over him, growling and menacing. The breeder stepped up and called him off.

"So now we know," said the policeman to the breeder. "Take the dog for a short walk, will you?" But the dog, it was clear, was not happy. He stood like a sentinel in front of his kennel, and it took more than the woman's persuasiveness to move him.

"What's he got in there?" she asked. "He wouldn't act like this unless he'd been put on guard." Without waiting for a reply, she said to the dog, "All right, then, good boy. Fetch!"

The dog went into the kennel and dragged out a heavy silver belt. He returned, but came out again and barked.

"He can't manage to fetch out the cups," said the policeman. "Billcaster was friends with the dog when he hid the stuff in the kennel, and then put him on guard. No wonder the dog turned savage when he thrashed him. He just couldn't understand the set-up. Could you, my beauty?" he concluded.

The Visitor

It was one of those seeping, sodden, misty, nasty evenings towards the middle of November. I had been out in the wet most of the day and now it was too dark to read and not quite dark enough for the lamps to be lit. There seemed nothing much to do except smoke a pipe at the fireside and wonder which of three invitations I should accept for Christmas.

Suddenly there was a quiet knock at the front door. Since my housekeeper would be in the middle of cooking my supper, and, in any case was as deaf as a post, I concluded that it was up to me to answer the door.

×

I groaned a little at the thought of a visitor. I had my reports to make up and some forms to fill in ready for the next day. However, I heaved myself out of my comfortable armchair and went along the passage. The caller was a stranger, a tall bearded chap who enquired for me by name.

"I'm Mr. Fairfield," I said. "What can I do for you?"

"You can get my roof mended," he replied.

"Roof? There's no roof in the village that wants repairing, so far as I know. But you'd better come in. Now then," I went on, when I had trimmed and lighted the two lamps in my small sitting-room. "I don't think I know you, and I thought I knew all the tenants on the estate."

"No, you don't know me," he agreed, "because I haven't settled in the village yet. But I've taken over old Williams's place, and the roof leaks plenty badly."

"Williams's place is freehold and his own. His roof is nothing to do with me. I only see about repairs for Sir Ralph's tenants. If you're not satisfied with the condition of the house you must tackle Williams about it."

"I see." He glanced round my room. "Snug little hole you've got here. They don't go in for luxuries like lodge-keepers in these hard times, I suppose?"

"No, otherwise I shouldn't be here. And now my housekeeper will soon be in with my evening meal, so if you'll excuse me ... "

"Just half a minute," he said. I hadn't asked him to sit down, and now, to my annoyance, he took his hands out of his pockets and pulled my old Windsor armchair nearer the fire. I suppose if I hadn't been sitting in it myself, he'd have had the upholstered one, which is far more comfortable! He sat down, began to warm his hands and went on: "See here, Mr. Fairfield, I've a proposition to make. If you'll see to this roof for me ... "

×

"By asking you to see to the roof, I don't mean make yourself responsible for the repairs," he said eagerly. "I only mean I wish you'd come along and have a look at it. Then you could advise me what to ask Williams to do. He's an old skinflint, and I'd like to be on safe ground with my demands so that he can't refuse them. As we're going to be neighbours I feel I've a right to ask such a trifling favour of you."

"I don't see it," I said, beginning to dislike him very much indeed. "I'm certainly not going to interfere in old Williams's affairs. For one thing, we're not on speaking terms."

"Oh, yes, I know there's bad blood between you," he announced. "It's common talk down at the pub. That's where I heard about your household arrangements, too. Well, what you won't do as a favour you'll have to do of necessity, that's all."

With that he lugged out an ugly little gun. "Would you mind putting your hands up? Sorry to trouble you and all that. That's right. Stay sitting right where you are."

×

"I'd like to tell you a short story. I used to live around these parts. Old Williams was a lot less old in those days. He got my sister into trouble. That was long before your time, of course.

"Now don't do anything rash, Mr. Fairfield, because if you do, and I have to shoot, it will bring old Maggie in here. She may be deaf, but she can't be as deaf as all that, and if she does come in I'll have to shoot her, too. You can see that, can't you? For one thing, she might remember me, and that wouldn't suit me at all."

"What about the chaps at the pubs?" I asked. "Didn't they recognise you? Some, at least, would be as old as you, and even older."

"A beard and a Canadian accent," he explained. "I'm staying at the pub, as a matter of fact, and get all the local news. Now you just stay put, Mr. Fairfield, and don't open that mouth of yours too wide, and I'll do you no harm."

"I thought you wanted me to come to Williams's place?" I said.

"I've changed my mind. It seems a pity to drag you out in all this rain. I'm sure you've had a hard day, and, by the sound, it's coming down in buckets. One thing, it should wash out any footprints I may have left."

"But to be on the safe side in going back, I wish ... " he motioned towards where my boots were drying ... "you'd change my shoes for me. Please be as quick as you can. It looks as if you take a size larger than I do, but nobody troubles to be dressy on a night like this."

I did as I was told. I also, at his request, put his own shoes into my game-bag, which was hanging from a nail in the wall, and slung it over his shoulder for him.

Then, still covering me, he took out a silk handkerchief and picked up my poker. I thought he was going to bat me over the head with it, but all he said was, as he backed towards the door, "Good lad! I'll be seeing you."

x

I did see him just once more. But that came some time later. That night, after he left me, old Williams was murdered. My poker, with my fingerprints on it, was found beside the body; my game-bag — empty — no shoes — was on a chair, and my muddy foot-prints were all over the stone floor of Williams's kitchen.

I had been heard in the pub when slightly under the influence, to utter sanguinary threats against Williams. All this could lead only to one thing ... my arrest on a charge of murder.

In vain I pleaded the truth and described the visit of the so-called Canadian. Old Maggie could not support my evidence. She had neither seen nor heard the man and she got confused about the time that she had brought me in my supper, the one bit of evidence that really would have helped me, since the time of Williams's death was fairly well agreed on by the doctors.

I was in despair. I could see no way in which to save myself. I was cautioned, charged, arrested, brought before the magistrate, and, finally, committed for trial.

x

Dyson, my solicitor, Sir Ralph, my employer, and poor old Maggie, my housekeeper, were the only people who believed in my innocence. Dyson, arranging for my defence, kept begging me to think. Was there not some proof that the murderer had been to my house that night? I racked my brains. Then came the inspiration.

"Good heavens. Of course," I said. "Look Dyson, I've just remembered. When he came into my sitting-room he sat down and hitched by Windsor armchair nearer the fire. I don't know why I didn't remember that before."

"Your Windsor armchair?"

"Man alive, yes. You know what a Windsor chair is like. It's made completely of wood. He took it by the arms and hitched it forward. If old Maggie has only kept to our agreement, the evidence of his fingerprints must still be there."

"Kept to your agreement?"

"That she was never to dust in there. She's a dear old thing, but stupid, and I've always got account books and papers about."

It was enough for Dyson. Off he went, to demand that the police should take the pseudo-Canadian's finger-prints and compare them with the ones they would find on the arms of my Windsor armchair.

But the police and the murderer between them did that one in. They were sufficiently impressed by Dyson to decide to take the fellow to my place and get him to have a look round. I don't know whether they thought he might possibly give himself away. The first thing he did, it seems, was to settle himself in the Windsor armchair and hitch it nearer the fire. He was pretty fly, that chap. He wasn't having any fingerprint dodges. He'd remembered.

But so did Maggie. She let the company out, poor Dyson most downcast and dejected. She pulled him by the sleeve and whispered hoarsely:

"Please, sir, that bearded gentleman. He've got the master's boots on. I'd know them anywhere. I've cleaned 'em so often."

×

They say a murderer always makes one mistake. This fellow was no exception. He'd had to get rid of his own shoes out of my game-bag, of course, and it turned out that he didn't possess another pair and had thought it too dangerous to attract attention in the shoe-shop by taking off a pair a size too large.

Oversight

"No, sir, I am not trying to frame you," said the inspector, patiently. "I am asking you to give me an account of what happened, and what your own part in it was. Cooperation, sir, is what I want, that's all."

The pig-faced young man snorted with discomfort and disbelief.

"That's all very well," he said, "and I'd help if I could, but I don't see what I can tell you that you don't know already."

"Something might come up, sir, some small point which wouldn't seem important, perhaps, to you, but which might help us quite a bit. I might tell you that we exercise considerable discretion with regard to potentially valuable witnesses, if that's what's troubling you."

"Discretion such as what?"

"Well, sir, such as that you might have left your driving license in the pocket of your other suit."

"Oh!" The young man's face flushed. He began to say something, changed his mind, swallowed and began again. "Oh, that. Yes, I see. Only it wasn't me, you know. It was my pal. He asked if he could drive for a bit, and it never occurred to me that he hadn't got his license on him, but when we spotted the copper we changed places.

"Unfortunately the bobby saw us and tried to stop us, but — well, I'm afraid I drove on past him."

"I see, sir. So that settles that. Well, now then. I think you can help me over what happened here last night."

"Fair enough. Here goes." The young man seemed relieved. He told his story briskly, and more impersonally than the inspector had expected, for his appearance, in the old-fashioned phrase, was against him.

"After I had crowded past the policeman we put a good 50 miles between him and ourselves. We had intended to put up at the Landsman's Trivet, but decided it was too close to the ... er ... incident, but I wish now we'd chanced it. A summons for side-stepping the copper would have been a sight more preferable than being mixed up in a case of murder."

"You both knew the murdered woman, I believe?"

"We'd seen her, that's all. It was in the saloon bar the night we got here. We had dinner and then passed on into the saloon bar and each had a large whisky. While we were there the head waiter came in and there was a bit of a row between him and the barmaid about some drinks."

×

"Could you hear the whole conversation, then?"

"Oh, yes, quite distinctly. There were two settees facing one another, with my pal and me in the corner of each, and the bar wasn't three yards away."

"Anybody else in the lounge?"

"No one at the time, no."

"What were you and your friend doing, besides dealing with your drinks?"

"Smoking. Cigars, if you want to know."

"You were not, then, conversing or reading?"

"No. We knew each other pretty well, and also we were both pretty tired. At least I know *I* was. Besides, I was still worried about dodging the policeman."

"So you listened intentionally to this dispute between the head waiter and the barmaid?"

"I don't know whether it was intentional, exactly, but, anyway, I couldn't help hearing what they said."

"Did you compare notes with your friend afterwards?"

"No. He hadn't heard a word. You see, he happens to be very deaf in the left ear, and that was the ear he had turned towards the bar."

"I see, sir. You said the quarrel was about some drinks. Can you give me the gist of what was said?"

"Hadn't you better ask the people concerned? I don't much like tales out of school."

"I have already interviewed them both, sir. I should, however, like to have your version of what was said."

"Don't their stories tally, then? Oh Lord! That makes things awkward."

"Why so, sir? We have to establish the truth. We don't want the wrong person hanged."

"No, of course not. But I can only give you the general impression, you know. No word-for-word business. I'm not prepared to swear an oath to anything of that sort."

"We should not expect it, sir. Of course not. Which of them began the quarrel?"

"The barmaid spoke first, but not in a quarreling way. She just said, 'Here's your slate for the month. Bill,' or something of that sort, and presented him with a slip of paper.

"He looked at it, swore under his breath (I think — it wasn't loud enough for me to catch) and crumpled the paper up and threw it into a fern-pot.

"He said, 'Don't be a gold-digger, Amy! I don't owe all that.' Then the girl said, 'Yes, you do, you old sponge!' But she still sounded quite bright.

"The chap leaned over and said, in a nasty sort of way, 'Don't you try to chisel me, you little such and such.' "

"And that, I suppose, began the quarrel?"

"You bet it did. She got as mad as a wet hen, went to a drawer at the back of the bar and pulled out a sort of long, thin notebook. She opened it and thumbed it through and then slapped it down on the counter in front of him. 'Take your change out of that, and take your sauce with you!' she said.

"But he wouldn't accept the account. Still said it was too big and that he knew he hadn't had as much as that, and he darned well wasn't going to pay.

"So she said very quietly, 'Either you or Miss Edna. Please yourself, dear.' "

"And then the fat was in the fire, I suppose."

"Then the fat was in the fire, inspector, as I don't mind telling you. In the end he did pay, but it was all pretty venomous. That's all I know. You could have knocked me down with a feather when I heard he'd killer her."

"I beg your pardon, sir? When you heard he'd killed her?"

"Oh, sorry, I thought that was what you were implying."

"Not necessarily, sir. Only, when we come upon the scene of a crime, especially murder, any disagreement between the persons involved, especially disagreement in their signed statements, is bound to be of interest."

"Could I ask what disagreement you noticed in their statements?"

"Why not? You have helped me considerably by your evidence. The chief point at issue seems to be that whilst you admit to the fact of the quarrel, the man concerned denies absolutely that they quarreled at all."

"Oh, but they did, you know, inspector. It was a very nasty row indeed. Rows about money usually are, I notice."

"It is a pity that your friend is unable to corroborate you, sir."

"You've already tackled him, I take it?"

"Not yet, sir. That will come later. If he is, as you say, stone deaf in one ear, it is unlikely that he will be able to help us very much.

×

"By the way, this little business of you and the constable, sir. I'd like to know more about that. It is unlikely that, in view of this murder business and the fact that you happened to be here at the time, the police will offer any charge against you as to driving on instead of stopping."

"Well, I must say that's good news, inspector. What's the catch in it?"

"That is for you to say, sir. May I take you over your statement? You affirm that when you saw the constable you thought you had better change seats with your friend and you yourself drive the car. That means you were certain that your friend had no driving license on him?

"I'll come clean about that, inspector. I knew he hadn't."

"Why shouldn't he have had one? I take it that you mean he did not possess a license."

"Since you put it that way, I agree that he didn't possess a license."

"And yet he could drive. You were quite willing to trust the car, and that might mean your life, to his driving."

"Well, yes at the part of the journey we had got to."

"I don't think I quite understand, sir."

"Well, it's simple enough, really. He hadn't been granted a license because the examiner found out that he was colour-blind."

"Colour-blind?"

"Yes. He mixed up red and green, as colour-blind men, I believe, so often do, so, of course, he couldn't be relied upon to read the traffic signals. But on the part of the road we had got to when we spotted the constable there were no traffic lights for miles."

"So you knew the road pretty well, sir."

"Well, of course I did, otherwise I should hardly have trusted him with the car, should I?"

Of course not, sir. I quite see that. Now, when you saw the constable you decided you had better change places. This was so that you could take the driver's seat. How did you convey this intention to your friend?"

"I think I muttered, 'Pull up, John! There's a copper. Switch over places, quick!' "

"You muttered this?"

"Yes, to save time, and to give him the impression it was urgent."

"You muttered this into the ear that was nearest you, naturally?"

"Well, I'd hardly have leaned all over him and muttered it into his other ear, would I?"

"I don't know, sir. If you'd had any sense or if you had been telling me the truth I should say that, yes, you would have leaned right over him. You say he was driving?"

"Yes. Otherwise there'd have been no point in us changing places."

×

"You also stated just now that he was deaf in the left ear. That is why he can't corroborate your report of the quarrel between the barmaid and the head waiter."

"Yes?" said the young man, looking puzzled. "I don't get your point, inspector."

"Rather odd, isn't it, sir, that if he is deaf in the left ear he could understand you when you muttered, whereas he couldn't hear what appears, according to you, to have been a perfectly audible quarrel. It isn't as though, seated side by side in the car as you obviously must have been, he could lip-read. People must of necessity be face-to-face for that."

"I still don't get you. What's all this about? I thought you told me ..."

"We don't need to arrest a man for driving past a constable when we can arrest him on a charge of murder," said the inspector drily. "I may add that we discover, on checking the hotel register, that you have stayed her several times before.

"Another point, although a small one. When I told you that stories of the quarrel told respectively by the barmaid and the head waiter did not agree, you made no attempt to point out to me that I could not possibly have got the barmaid's story of that quarrel since she was the murdered woman.

"What your connection with her could have been, or why you should have killed her, I don't yet know. But it is my duty to tell you that you are now under arrest for the murder of Amy Aline Smith, and that anything you may say will be taken down in writing and may be used as evidence."

The Manuscript

"We've got to get him," said the Superintendent, "and it's up to you, Rogers. The motive, to a man of his sort, must have loomed up like a mountain. He's a fanatic and almost a recluse, which means he's no sense of proportion.

"After all, it happened to Thomas Carlyle to finish writing a book and then have the manuscript accidentally burned. And that was an important book, mark you, not like this tripe of old Besley's."

"A book about prison life, wasn't it? — Besley's, I mean."

"Yes. He got his stuff direct from the horse's mouth. Used to offer the old lags jobs when they came out and suck them dry. Then he'd write them the whale of a character, sack them gently and politely, and take on another bird of the same kidney."

"Feather, sir. Well, what made him change his habits and kill this girl instead of firing her?"

"Simply that she seems to have taken exception to the circumstances in which she found herself, and chucked the whole manuscript on the fire. She wasn't really an old lag, you see. It appears that he'd finished the big section devoted to men criminals and wanted to put in an extra bit about women. Well, he'd already engaged a woman baby-farmer who'd received a life-sentence and had been released on a good-conduct remission, and he wanted a first offender for contrast.

"He picked this girl Angie, who said she was only too ready to go straight, treated her kindly, talked to her about her experiences and, from what we can gather from her relations — all more or less of criminal character, incidentally, he rehabilitated her in her own eyes until she was almost ready to worship him. We've got all this from the letters she used to write home. Then, in accordance with his custom, he gave her the sack. When she protested, the old brute came clean and told her what he had really wanted her for. The idea that her misdeeds were to be handed down to posterity seemed to upset her.

"She sneaked down at night when she knew he had gone to bed, broke open his writing desk, collared the manuscript and stoked the kitchen fire with it. We know all this because she wrote to her parents and told them what she had done."

"And how long after she'd burned the book and written the letter —?"

"Two days. It chanced that he spent the first day fixing up with the next ex-prisoner he wanted, name of Nelly, a girl of Angie's age who was being released after serving a sentence for gang crimes. Besley brought her back with him, and finding Angie still there, inveigled her into the woods outside his house and did her in — in other words, broke her neck.

"She'd been killed where she was found, moreover. That's our difficulty. There's nothing to show that he ever went out of the house, and the new girl, Nelly can't help us. At least, she says she can't."

"Who found the body?"

"A gamekeeper, out after grey squirrels. It appears they inhabit those woods and every so often he goes after them with a gun."

"Could it possibly have been an accident?"

"No, I don't see that it could. She'd collected a punch on the jaw."

×

Detective-inspector Rogers went off to see Besley. He turned out to be a bearded, crafty-looking gentleman on the threshold of old-age. Rogers sized him up but could scarcely see him as the deliverer of murderous blows. He suddenly said: "Do you mind if I look at your hands, sir?"

The recluse stretched them out. Those fine-skinned knuckles had never, unaided, dealt death-blow to a healthy girl. So much Rogers saw at once.

Rogers went off to look at the place where the girl had been found dead. A local constable was posted just outside the area, which was cordoned off with ropes. Rogers produced his authority, and they chatted.

"Nothing else come to light, I suppose?"

"Nothing at all, sir."

"H'm. Leaf-mould everywhere. That means no identifiable footprints. And no weapon except somebody's fist. All right, constable."

He walked back to the house and found Besley, glasses on nose, bent industriously over his papers. "I've begun my book again, you see. Just like Carlyle, I've kept all my case notes, I find."

"That's very fortunate, sir," said Rogers. This, he regretted, did away with the motive. He inspected the manuscripts from which Besley had been working. So far as he could tell, they were genuine case-notes.

"Were you very angry when you found the girl had burned your manuscript?" he asked.

"I was, indeed," said Besley. "But I simmered down, you know."

"Now, listen, Mr. Besley. You didn't know your book was destroyed when you went to engage this girl Nelly? — No, I thought not. What did you know about Nelly?"

"Well," said Besley, "I knew of course that she had been mixed up with a gang. She was terrified of her old associates, too. She seems frightened out of her life."

"Ah, yes. All right, Mr. Besley. I shan't need to bother you again. Perhaps I could have just a word with Nelly"

x

"But what gave you the clue?" demanded the Superintendent. "We've picked up Nelly's boyfriend, on your instructions."

"I couldn't believe he killed the girl," said Rogers. "For one thing, with those hands of his, I couldn't see it happening — but, from the medical evidence, he didn't. But it was clearly to the advantage of the rest of her gang that Nelly's activities should remain anonymous. Once her story was down in black and white not one of them felt himself safe. They must have picketed the house, and, as Angie fled from old Besley's wrath, one of them mistook her for Nelly — quite an easy thing in the gloom of the woods at evening."

The Fish-Pond

Potter, the laboratory assistant, made up his mind to kill Mr. Sikes, the science master. He had disliked Sikes for months, and this dislike turned to hatred when one day Sikes rebuked him very harshly and, as it turned out, unjustly, in front of a group of boys.

Potter, 40 years old, felt it keenly. It rankled and fettered in his mind.

At the start of the summer term Sikes announced to Potter that the school fish-pond needed to be cleaned out. This fish-pond was one of Mr. Sikes's hobbies. It had been constructed, under his directions, by boys of the middle school seven years previously, and rare plants had been imported and solemnly installed in it. Also it had received a present of a dozen small fish.

Potter listened in moody silence while Sikes outlined such details as he wished Potter to observe in cleaning the pond. Potter had heard it all a good many times before. If one thing was needed to bolster his determination to get rid of the master, that high-pitched, nervous voice would have provided it.

"And those things Kew Gardens sent us," Mr. Sikes concluded. "I'll shift those myself when you've taken the fish out and drained the water off, so be sure you send for me before you begin the cleaning."

"Very good, sir," growled Potter, "but I shan't need to send. I'll come my own self. I don't want no boys to help me. More trouble than they're worth."

"Very well, please yourself."

"Which day shall I be cleaning out the pond, sir?"

"Since you won't require boys to help you you had better make it Saturday. I've got to be here to set up some experiments for the Fifth Form for Monday morning, so I shall be able to supervise the pond at the same time."

x

It was unfair of Mr. Sikes to choose a Saturday, and Potter knew it — he was supposed to have all Saturday off. But this time he rejoiced. The school would be closed, and nobody except himself, Mr. Sikes and the school caretaker would be about. He perfected his plans that night.

First he collected and carefully smashed half a dozen bottles of various shapes, sizes and thicknesses of glass. The jagged pieces he put into his old attaché case, carried them to the school premises next day and hid them in his little den which opened off the laboratory.

He returned to the school that evening while it was still daylight and after the caretaker had gone off duty, removed the fish to the laboratory aquarium and then partly drained the pond by dipping in empty buckets used by the cleaners. When sufficient water was out, he packed his jagged glass very carefully — wearing a pair of leather gloves so that he did not cut himself — round the roots, deep in the ooze of the precious water-plants which the master was to lift next day, and poured back the water.

×

Next morning Potter went along to the laboratory for the cleaning-out implements he would require, and paused to look at the aquarium in which he had placed the fish. Here he received a slight shock. There should have been twelve fish, but he could only count ten. Two must still be in the pond.

When he got down to the pond he noticed that the water had cleared quite nicely, but there were the two missing fish, dead, and floating bloatedly on the surface. Potter swore, removed them, and hid them in a small rockery which bounded one side of the pond. Then he drained off the water. When nothing but ooze and the water-plants remained, he walked over to the building to summon Sikes.

"There we are, sir," he said in his usual lugubrious tones. "I could have lifted that there Kew Gardens stuff myself, but seeing as how you said you wanted me to call you — "

"Yes, yes. Leave it to me," said Sikes peevishly. "I suppose you got all the fish out?"

"Oh, yes, sir. I got them all."

×

Mr. Sikes grunted and knelt upon the grass. He thrust his hands well down into the mud which held the water-plants firm, but withdrew them with an exclamation of horror. They were badly gashed, and were smothered in blood and mud. The next instant he had tumbled forward faint with pain and fear. He had a phobia, as Potter knew well, about tetanus, and was for ever warning his boys against getting soil into cuts.

This faintness was Potter's chance, and he had banked on it.

Quickly he turned on this hose to refill the pond, then he leaped on the prostrate man and cruelly forced his head down into the rising water. He did not fill the pond up.

As soon as he knew that Mr. Sikes was dead he turned off the hose, went back into school and deliberately sought out the school caretaker. They smoked cigarettes in the caretaker's little den down among the boilers, and then Potter suggested that Mr. Sikes must have lifted the plants and he supposed that he had better be getting back to begin the cleaning. A moment later he was back, breathless, to report that Mr. Sikes was drowned. The police were at the school within five minutes of the caretaker's telephone call, and a doctor followed immediately.

Both doctor and police were interested in the terrible gashes in the dead man's hands. They asked Potter about them.

"Them rats of boys, I expect," he growled. "Can't keep upsides with what they gets up to."

The police poked and probed, doing disastrous damage to the water–plants and to the rockery. Soon they discovered the packed broken glass and the two dead fish. Potter had overlooked these fish, but did not see how they could incriminate him. He explained their presence by saying that he had found them dead when he went along to empty the pond, and had tossed them aside, thinking to get rid of them later.

The police pointed out that the fish had not been tossed aside, but carefully hidden. They sent the fish for analysis.

When the analyst's report came back, it showed that the fish had died from swallowing mud instead of water. The analyst was also able to establish that the fish must have been dead about 15 hours when the police discovered them.

×

The police inspector questioned Potter carefully.

"You say that Mr. Sikes was too impatient to let you finish emptying the pond before he took up the plants. Yet two fish died of a sort of fishy asphyxia. You've looked after this pond for seven years, and yet cannot explain how this happened. I suggest you emptied the pond on the previous night, packed in that broken glass, and did not notice that two fish had got themselves buried in the mud."

Potter denied this vigorously, but the inspector had not finished. The newly checked beakers and test tubes provided plenty of fingerprints. Potter's were taken — he could scarcely refuse if he wanted to be thought an innocent man. He had forgotten that water — even running water — does not necessarily wash out fingerprints which are always oily. Those pieces of glass which Sikes had not handled bore every one of them the evidence of Potter's fingers.

Alibi

"Oh, yes," said the detective, "it has been tried in real life. Why it was tried on me once, by a couple of women who happened to be pretty well identical twins."

×

One was a childless widow, the other a spinster, when they were about 40 years old they went into service with a wealthy old bachelor named Peacock. They were hard-working and competent, and after they had looked after Peacock for several years they learned that a couple of thousand pounds was to come their way when he died, provided that they were still in his service. The rest was to go to a great-niece who used to look after him when the sisters took their annual summer holiday.

They used to go off for a fortnight at the beginning of June, usually to a big hotel which, on their wages, they could afford. As they said, it made a complete change for them from their ordinary life. They chose a different hotel each time, and probably had a lot of fun pretending to be people of leisure.

On this occasion they went to Larcombe, to a very big hotel right on the front called Flowerdew. They booked, as usual, a double room with twin beds, but on the appointed day only one of them turned up.

She had — we got these details later, of course — a brown suitcase, wore a brown hat and costume, and carried a grey waterproof. She signed the hotel register as Mrs. Kimmer, and said that her sister would be coming later by train. She was given the key of the double room, the porter took up her luggage, she had a wash and went in to lunch. After lunch she went out, and about an hour later a woman exactly like her appeared.

She signed the register as Miss Crass, had a blue silk scarf on her head, wore a light summer coat, had a blue umbrella and a blue suitcase. They key, which had been handed in, was given her, the porter took up her luggage, she remarked to him that she supposed lunch was over but that she had had something on the train, and remained in the bedroom to unpack.

At tea-time she reappeared and had tea in the lounge. Then she handed in the key at the office, remarking that her sister would want it when she changed for dinner, and went out. At just after six the brown-clad woman came back, asked for the key and whether her sister had arrived, went up, changed, had a light dinner of soup, fish and ice-cream, and went into the lounge for coffee.

×

Now it so happens that at the Flowerdew there is a door from the lounge to the saloon bar and so to the street, therefore the comings and goings of guests are not always remarked by the office staff. What is certain on that particular evening, however, is that, a little later, the blue woman went into the dining-room and had a meal of soup, joint and two vegetables, a soufflé, and coffee at the table.

She remarked to the waiter that she supposed her sister had already dined, and added, “I don’t suppose you’ll see us together much in here. We’ve had a bit of a tiff.”

When the chambermaid went in to tidy the room next morning, both beds had been used. At 12 o’clock a telegram was delivered at the hotel directed to Mrs. Kimmer. She was paged and the lad found her in the lounge drinking gin and orange.

She tore open the telegram, gasped (said the lad), and exclaimed: “Good heavens! This is terrible. Take this to the office and tell them to show it to my sister directly she comes in. And get me my bill at once, and bring it up to Number Thirty.”

She paid her bill, begged them to be sure to show the telegram to her sister as soon as she came back from her walk, and said, “Tell her I’ve left a note for her in our room. I expect she’ll want to follow me at once.”

Then she got the porter to ring for a taxi, and drove to the railway station. Soon afterwards the blue woman came in, and was intercepted by the page.

The blue woman threw it down when she had seen it, gave a slight scream, and exclaimed, “The wicked, wicked creature! The minute we leave that poor old man. Quick, my bill.”

She rushed upstairs while they were making it out, came down a few minutes later, blue suitcase in hand, paid the bill, refused the porter’s offer to get a taxi, and careered off.

Up to this point the alibi — you understand, of course, that the brown and the blue ladies were not two ladies but only one — was perfect.

Then a curious thing happened. Soon after the blue woman had left the hotel, a second telegram was delivered, also for Mrs. Kimmer. Not knowing quite what to do with it, the office staff opened it with the intention (so they told us, and it may be true) of telephoning its contents to Mrs. Kimmer's address as soon as they thought she might have arrived home. This second telegram read: "Dreadful news come at once." The first telegram had said: "Uncle killed return immediately." The signature in each case was Peacock.

Well, the hotel staff thought this very odd, but they accounted for it by supposing that two different people related to "Uncle" had telegraphed each being unaware that the other had done so. But when we came to investigate, this explanation did not hold water. The great-niece was the old man's only living relative and she had sent the second telegram but not the first one.

×

Well, we started by finding out about Mr. Peacock — who had, of course, been murdered. The great-niece told us that at four o'clock on the afternoon of the day that the twin sisters were supposed to have gone on holiday she had taken the old gentleman his tea. Then she had gone to the cinema. She returned at about eight o'clock to find him with his head smashed in and the coal-hammer lying beside him. Its handle had been wiped clear of fingerprints.

We suspected her strongly at first. She stood to gain so much more from his death than anybody else did, and money is always a big motive for murder. On the other hand, she had undoubtedly gone to the pictures. We satisfied ourselves about that; no funny business about tickets or going out in the middle of the performance unnoticed or anything of that kind.

×

So we turned our attention to the two sisters. I went down to Larcombe and inspected those telegrams. Then I got descriptions of the senders.

One description tallied with the age and appearance of the niece ... that was at the post office nearest the house. The other was sent from a post office a good deal further away, by someone who did not sound at all like the niece. It did not take us long to satisfy ourselves that the sender of the first telegram had been one of the twins, the one who stayed behind and did the murder.

It was obvious, of course, that the Box and Cox business could not be carried on indefinitely at the hotel. The murder had to be done without delay and the other sister recalled. It had been overlooked by these women that the niece would inevitably send for them herself. That was their first oversight.

The second was as big a mistake, and it was pointed out by that sharp-eyed page-boy. He had noticed that neither woman wore a wedding-ring.

As for the changes of clothing, it was easy enough to hire a beach hut and await a convenient opportunity to change from one set of outdoor garments to another.

The Vacuum Cleaner

Percy Perrier, the novelist, hated the vacuum cleaner from the moment it made its appearance in his home.

He had always said that nothing was too good for his wife, but the sweeper made him qualify this. He had only bought the thing because she was depressed over the death of their dog. The cleaner was noisy and interrupted his work. It consumed expensive electric current. It was much dearer than a dog-license. He began to brood about it instead of getting on with his novel. He had visions of smashing it up. Then he thought of what it had cost and of what his wife would say.

At time went on he detested it more and more. It got between him and his novel, between him and his food. He had indigestion; he could not sleep at nights. He decided that, wife or no wife, the sweeper must be put out of action.

×

He bided his time. Came the spring, and the spring-cleaning, during which he went away to the sea. This had been the arrangement for years. While his wife and the charwoman washed, scrubbed, polished, swept, took picnic meals off the floor and generally turned the house into something like a little hell upon earth, he was basking in April sunshine or tramping sturdily happy, in April rain.

But this year the week's break seemed different. He had never noticed before that the hotel staff began to vacuum-clean the landing outside his bedroom door at half-past six in the morning. This time it got on his nerves to such an extent that he found himself waking up at five and waiting for the noise to begin. He even went to the length of complaining. The manager merely shrugged his handsome shoulders and said he was very sorry, but he could not get women to work in the old-fashioned way with brush and dustpan anymore; it was hard enough to get them as it was. Besides, electric-cleaners were hygienic: the brush and dustpan method was not. He drew pictures of consumptive charwomen of bronchial hall-porters of guests with hacking coughs.

Perrier returned to a clean, rearranged home, with an exhausted, nervy wife. "Mother" she said, "has invited us for a week, but I said I didn't think you could go, as you'd got to catch up with your novel. She seemed rather upset, so I said I'd go by myself. You could manage for a week with Mrs. Miles to come in and cook for you, couldn't you darling?"

"Of course, of course. You look really knocked up, my dear. A week away from it all will do you no end of good."

It would do him no end of good, too, he thought. A whole week with no vacuum cleaner going.

He saw his wife off at the railway station. Then he came home, took the vacuum cleaner from its neat box, and studied it closely. He decided that he had better try it in order to come upon the best way of putting it out of action. By the time he put it away he had swept every carpet in the house. He was amazed to find how quickly the time had gone by.

×

His wife returned home and almost immediately contracted influenza. She stayed in bed, the doctor was sent for, and the upshot was that Perrier arranged to do all the housework with the aid of the vacuum cleaner if the charwoman would cook the meals and look after his wife. Then his wife complained that the cleaner was driving her mad.

"I've always hated the noise," she said fretfully. "I only used the thing to please you because you bought it for me. While you were away we did everything by hand."

Perrier dashed downstairs, picked up the whole contraption and strode out into the garden. He took the sweeper apart. Then he told the charwoman to go. He went to his tool-shed for fork and spade and dug a large grave in which to bury the sweeper and its attachments. Whilst he was thus employed, a man known to the police as Corgi Harry reconnoitered the house. He had seen the charwoman go out, and had spent a week or two in the guise of a window-cleaner working the neighbourhood. He propped his ladder against the front bedroom window, pulled up the sash and dropped in. Mrs. Perrier heard him and began to turn round in the bed.

The thief leaped at her in a panic. She caught a strong smell of aniseed as he brought a stick down on her head. The sight of her blood terrified him. He struck again, and then, without attempting to carry out his intention of robbing the house, he made his escape.

About two hours later Perrier, much the better for his strenuous work, came back from the garden, went upstairs to make his peace with his wife, and found her unconscious.

x

The doctor took a grave view of Mrs. Perrier. The police took an even graver view of Perrier. The grave in the garden was there for all to see; the wife was unconscious. The police arrested him and charged him with assault with intent to murder. They listened to his story in silence.

The only person who believed his story was the charwoman, Mrs. Miles. She reiterated: "It was the sweeper he was mad with, not with the missus or me."

Then Mrs. Perrier got better. She made a statement to the police in which she said: "I heard a noise at the window. We never have a window-cleaner. Mrs. Miles does it. She sits out on the sill. I don't like it much, but Percy can't do the windows. He can't even mount a step-ladder. He never has. Heights make him dreadfully dizzy. All I remember is terrible smell of aniseed."

"Corgi Harry," exclaimed the police inspector suddenly. "We heard he was working the neighbourhood. Nothing taken. Just like him to bolt at the sight of blood."

"She couldn't have invented that smell of aniseed, sir," his sergeant pointed out. "Pity Corgi Harry hadn't had his trousers cleaned."

"From his point of view, it's a pity he didn't stick to dog-stealing," said the inspector.

Arsenic in the House ...

It was going to be a simple matter, Brighton decided. The arsenic had been easy enough to obtain. Its administration would not be difficult. Sophie was addicted to black coffee, which would make a good vehicle for the poison.

The only problem was that she had never been known to suffer from any form of gastric illness, and gastritis, as he well knew, was the alibi of the arsenic poisoner. Unless Sophie had a previous history of serious indigestion it would be difficult, if not impossible, to obtain a death certificate with (so to speak) no questions asked, and the doctor duly signing on the dotted line.

Then the great idea dawned on him. Why bother with arsenic at all? It was a two-edged sword, as others before him had found out.

No, there was a better, a safer way. A hint dropped here, a saloon-bar confidence given there and few people in his immediate neighbourhood could fail, in the end, to learn of Sophie's extraordinary habit of sleeping with her head under the pillow instead of on it. Further hints and further confidences would build up in the minds of cronies and neighbours a picture of a household divided on the question of the danger of this practice. If it came to Sophie's ears that he was spreading these rumours her reaction, he knew, would be to laugh heartily. She was a very hearty woman altogether.

x

A year of pretended mourning for her, and quiet little Celia would be a pleasant change.

Unfortunately for Brighton there was one person in the little town who became thoughtful over these reports of Sophie's sleeping habits.

That person was a young dispenser at the local hospital. His name was Simms. He was not a frequent visitor to the saloon bar of the Crown, but he did happen to be there on more than one evening when Brighton was regaling friends with a vivid report of how he had been awakened by the sound of Sophie's loud snortings and of how he had been only just in time to save her life, and of how something ought to be done about it.

×

Young Simms disliked what he had seen and heard of Brighton but believed that the man was genuinely worried. He thought matters over as he walked back to his lodgings one night and decided to confide in a woman dispenser with whom he was on "dinner and show" terms. His friends would find something humorous, he fancied. In the story of a self-destructive wife who, prevented from unconsciously attempted suicide, hurled the means of her destruction at her interfering husband — she had hurled the pillow wildly at Brighton, it appeared — but Kay would listen and not laugh.

Kay did listen and, although she also laughed a little, she saw that the conscientious Simms was anxious and so she said sensibly: "I wonder whether this Brighton has told the doctor how his wife sleeps? It almost seems as though he ought to."

"That's an idea! I'll ask him. He always seems to be at the Crown."

He reported back to Kay on the following day over lunch at the hospital canteen. "He says her doctor does know and doesn't think anything of it, but I should have thought she ought to be frightened out of it."

"Well, as long as the doctor knows, I suppose it's all right," said Kay.

×

They left it at that, but Brighton turned over young Simms's question in his mind and came to the conclusion that any doctor called in to view the murdered Sophie would begin by putting the same question.

The thought preyed upon Brighton's mind. He no longer talked of pillows to his cronies, but of indigestion. At last, he said, he had persuaded Sophie to sleep with her pillow in the normal position, but it seemed to have upset her inside, and this so seriously that he had begun to wonder whether he had done the right thing after all.

×

Simms, who continued from time to time his visits to the Crown, could not help thinking that Sophie's indigestion was a very interesting symptom of what must be a deep psychological disturbance. So he said to Brighton one evening in the Crown: "Does she take anything for it — or is it just nerves?"

"For what?" asked Brighton, startled at being addressed for the second time by this young nosy-parker who had caused him to alter his plans.

"Her indigestion, you know. The tummy upset. I'm a dispenser. If you'd like me to recommend anything — she ought to see a doctor, though, really. If anything is seriously wrong — I mean, one never knows. It's always wisest not to take chances. A duodenal — I mean. I don't want to seem interfering, but, well, dispensing is my job."

Brighton thanked him in a strangled voice, finished his drink and went home.

He was utterly unprepared for what he found. Sophie was dead. She had been very sick.

At first he was stunned. Then he felt incredulous about his good luck. Then he rejoiced in it. He went to the telephone box at the end of the road and called her doctor.

x

The doctor looked grave and refused to give a death certificate.

Brighton had anticipated this. He was not even surprised when the doctor ordered a postmortem. But he was both surprised and shocked when a detective-inspector called upon him. Sophie had died from poisoning by arsenic.

The net closed quickly. In vain did he plead that the death was a suicide. The purchase of the weed-killer was soon traced to him. His saloon-bar confidences told heavily against him. Young Simms volunteered a statement that Brighton had carefully paved the way for the death by referring to his wife's indigestion.

x

Brighton was brought to trial. There was no evidence in his favour. It turned out (a circumstance he had overlooked) that Sophie had often visited her sister, who lived alone and had a small flat with one bedroom which the two women had shared. It was on oath that the sister declared that Sophie had never slept with a pillow over her face; that she had never suffered from any form of indigestion.

What Sophie *had* suffered from (but even her sister did not know this) was the feeling that Brighton had tired of her. She knew that he had bought the weed-killer and in a fit of despair she had taken her own life.

The jury were out for less than half an hour. They did not look at the prisoner when they came back.

Sources

"The Case of the Hundred Cats." *The* [London] *Evening Standard* [hereafter *ES*], 17 August 1936; *Fifty Famous Detectives of Fiction*, Odhams n.d. (1938); *Ladies in Crime*, Faber 1947.
"Daisy Bell." *Detective Stories of Today*, Faber 1940; *Crime on Her Mind*, Joseph 1976.
"Strangers' Hall." *ES*, 17 January 1950; *The Evening Standard Detective Book*, Gollancz 1950.
"A Light on Murder." *ES*, 15 February 1950; *The Evening Standard Detective Book*, Gollancz 1950.
"Rushy Glen." *ES*, 5 June 1950.
"Juniper Gammon." *ES*, 14 June 1950.
"Manor Park." *ES*, 18 August 1950; *The Evening Standard Detective Book*, series 2, Gollancz 1951; variant text in *The Third Bedside Book of Great Detective Stories*, Barker 1978. [We have used the *ES* version.]
"The Jar of Ginger." *ES*, 28 September 1950; *The Evening Standard Detective Book*, series 2, Gollancz 1951.
"The Knife." *ES*, 11 January 1951.
"Practical Joke." *ES*, 19 January 1951.
"Our Pageant." *ES*, 19 September 1951.
"The Tree." *ES*, 21 September 1951.
"Sammy." *ES*, 29 September 1951.
"Peach Jam." *ES*, 6 November 1951.
"The Plumb-Line." *ES*, 13 November 1951.
"Haunted House." *ES*, 9 February 1952.
"The Falling Petals." *ES*, 6 March 1952.
"The Price of Lead." *ES*, 6 June 1952.
"The Spell." *ES*, 14 June 1952.
"A Bit of Garden." *ES*, 18 June 1952.
"The Swimming Gala." *ES*, 25 July 1952.
"The Tooth-Pick." *ES*, 3 October 1952.
"The Bodkin." *ES*, 11 October 1952.
"The Boxer." *ES*, 17 January 1953.
"The Visitor." *ES*, 4 February 1953.
"Oversight." *ES*, 13 February 1953.
"The Manuscript." *ES*, 11 May 1953.
"The Fish-Pond." *ES*, 19 May 1953.
"Alibi." *ES*, 23 May 1953.
"The Vacuum Cleaner." *ES*, 2 July 1953.
"Arsenic in the House . . ." *ES*, 6 June 1956.

Sleuth's Alchemy

Sleuth's Alchemy: Cases of Mrs. Bradley and Others by Gladys Mitchell, edited by Nicholas Fuller, is set in 12-point Garamond and printed on 60 pound natural shade opaque acid-free paper. The cover illustration is by Gail Cross, and the Lost Classics design is by Deborah Miller. *Sleuth's Alchemy* was published in January 2005 by Crippen & Landru Publishers, Norfolk, Virginia.

CRIPPEN & LANDRU, PUBLISHERS
P. O. Box 9315
Norfolk, VA 23505
E-mail: info@crippenlandru.com
www.crippenlandru.com

Crippen & Landru publishes first editions of short-story collections by important detective and mystery writers.

☞This is the best edited, most attractively packaged line of mystery books introduced in this decade. The books are equally valuable to collectors and readers. [*Mystery Scene Magazine*]

☞The specialty publisher with the most star-studded list is Crippen & Landru, which has produced short story collections by some of the biggest names in contemporary crime fiction. [*Ellery Queen's Mystery Magazine*]

☞God Bless Crippen & Landru. [*The Strand Magazine*]

☞A monument in the making is appearing year by year from Crippen & Landru, a small press devoted exclusively to publishing the criminous short story. [*Alfred Hitchcock's Mystery Magazine*]

LOST CLASSICS

Crippen & Landru is proud to publish a series of *new* short-story collections by great authors of the past who specialized in traditional mysteries. Each book collects stories from crumbling pages of old pulp, digest, and slick magazines, and most of the stories have been "lost" since their first publication. The following books are in print:

The Newtonian Egg and Other Cases of Rolf le Roux by Peter Godfrey, introduction by Ronald Godfrey. 2002. Trade softcover, $15.00.

Murder, Mystery and Malone by Craig Rice, edited by Jeffrey A. Marks. 2002. Trade softcover, $19.00.

The Sleuth of Baghdad: The Inspector Chafik Stories, by Charles B. Child. Cloth, $27.00. 2002. Trade softcover, $17.00.

Hildegarde Withers: Uncollected Riddles by Stuart Palmer, introduction by Mrs. Stuart Palmer. 2002. Cloth, $29.00. Trade softcover, $19.00.

The Spotted Cat and Other Mysteries from the Casebook of Inspector Cockrill by Christianna Brand, edited by Tony Medawar. 2002. Cloth, $29.00. Trade softcover, $19.00.

Marksman and Other Stories by William Campbell Gault, edited by Bill Pronzini; afterword by Shelley Gault. 2003. Trade softcover, $19.00.

Karmesin: The World's Greatest Criminal — Or Most Outrageous Liar by Gerald Kersh, edited by Paul Duncan. 2003. Cloth, $27.00. Trade softcover, $17.00.

The Complete Curious Mr. Tarrant by C. Daly King, introduction by Edward D. Hoch. 2003. Cloth, $29.00. Trade softcover, $19.00.

The Pleasant Assassin and Other Cases of Dr. Basil Willing by Helen McCloy, introduction by B.A. Pike. 2003. Cloth, $27.00. Trade softcover, $18.00.

Murder – All Kinds by William L. DeAndrea, introduction by Jane Haddam. 2003. Cloth, $29.00. Trade softcover, $19.00.

The Avenging Chance and Other Mysteries from Roger Sheringham's Casebook by Anthony Berkeley, edited by Tony Medawar and Arthur Robinson. 2004. Cloth, $29.00. Trade softcover, $19.00.

Banner Deadlines: The Impossible Files of Senator Brooks U. Banner by Joseph Commings, edited by Robert Adey; memoir by Edward D. Hoch. 2004. Cloth, $29.00. Trade softcover, $19.00.

The Danger Zone and Other Stories by Erle Stanley Gardner, edited by Bill Pronzini. 2004. Cloth, $29.00. Trade softcover, $19.00.

Dr. Poggioli: Criminologist by T.S. Stribling, edited by Arthur Vidro. Cloth, $29.00. 2004. Trade softcover, $19.00.

The Couple Next Door: Collected Short Mysteries by Margaret Millar, edited by Tom Nolan. 2004. Trade softcover, $19.00.

Sleuth's Alchemy: Cases of Mrs. Bradley and Others by Gladys Mitchell, edited by Nicholas Fuller. 2004. Cloth, $29.00. Trade softcover, $19.00.

Who Was Guilty? Two Dime Novels by Philip S. Warne/Howard W. Macy, edited by Marlena E. Bremseth. 2004. Cloth, $29.00. Trade softcover, $19.00.

Slot-Machine Kelly by Michael Collins, introduction by Robert J. Randisi. Cloth, $29.00. 2004. Trade softcover, $19.00.

The Evidence of the Sword by Rafael Sabatini, edited by Jesse F. Knight. 2006. Cloth, $29.00. Trade softcover, $19.00.

The Casebook of Sidney Zoom by Erle Stanley Gardner, edited by Bill Pronzini. 2006. Trade softcover, $19.00.

The Detections of Francis Quarles by Julian Symons, edited by John Cooper; afterword by Kathleen Symons. 2006. Cloth, $29.00. Trade softcover, $19.00.

The Trinity Cat and Other Mysteries by Ellis Peters (Edith Pargeter), edited by Martin Edwards and Sue Feder. 2006. Trade softcover, $19.00.

The Grandfather Rastin Mysteries by Lloyd Biggle, Jr., edited by Kenneth Lloyd Biggle and Donna Biggle Emerson. 2007. Cloth, $29.00. Trade softcover, $19.00.

Masquerade: Ten Crime Stories by Max Brand, edited by William F. Nolan. 2007. Cloth, $29.00. Trade softcover, $19.00.

Dead Yesterday and Other Mysteries by Mignon G. Eberhart, edited by Rick Cypert and Kirby McCauley. Cloth, $30.00. Trade softcover, $20.00.

FORTHCOMING LOST CLASSICS

The Battles of Jericho by Hugh Pentecost, introduction by S.T. Karnick

The Minerva Club, The Department of Patterns and Other Stories by Victor Canning, edited by John Higgins

The Casebook of Gregory Hood by Anthony Boucher and Denis Green, edited by Joe R. Christopher

The Casebook of Jonas P. Jonas and Others by Elizabeth Ferrars, edited by John Cooper

Ten Thousand Blunt Instruments by Philip Wylie, edited by Bill Pronzini.

Erle Stanley Gardner, *The Exploits of the Patent Leather Kid*, edited by Bill Pronzini.

Vincent Cornier, *Duel of Shadows*, edited by Mike Ashley.

Phyllis Bentley, *Author in Search of a Character: The Detections of Miss Phipps*, edited by Marvin Lachman.

Balduin Groller, *Detective Dagobert: Master Sleuth of Old Vienna*, translated by Thomas Riediker.

SUBSCRIPTIONS

Crippen & Landru offers discounts to individuals and institutions who place Standing Order Subscriptions for its forthcoming publications, either all the Regular Series or all the Lost Classics or (preferably) both. Collectors can thereby guarantee receiving limited editions, and readers won't miss any favorite stories. Standing Order Subscribers receive a specially commissioned story in a deluxe edition as a gift at the end of the year. Please write or e-mail for more details.

Lost Classics

Printed in the United States
147099LV00003B/6/A

9 781932 009316